John L. Davies

Order and Growth

as involved in the spiritual constitution of human society

John L. Davies

Order and Growth
as involved in the spiritual constitution of human society

ISBN/EAN: 9783337332334

Printed in Europe, USA, Canada, Australia, Japan

Cover: Foto ©Andreas Hilbeck / pixelio.de

More available books at **www.hansebooks.com**

ORDER AND GROWTH

AS INVOLVED
IN THE SPIRITUAL CONSTITUTION
OF HUMAN SOCIETY

BY THE

REV. J. LLEWELYN DAVIES, M.A.,

CHAPLAIN TO THE QUEEN;

VICAR OF KIRKBY LONSDALE; FORMERLY FELLOW OF TRINITY COLLEGE, CAMBRIDGE

London

MACMILLAN AND CO.

AND NEW YORK

1891

PREFACE

THIS book consists in the main of the Hulsean Lectures delivered at Cambridge in the year 1890.

If it has the good fortune to prove itself helpful to any readers, it will be, I believe, through the account which it gives of the nature of the Church, and of Justice. The ideas which I have endeavoured to expound on these subjects do not claim to be original, but they are not so familiar to Christians in general as—if I am right—they ought to be. And there must be many whom the current descriptions both of the Church and of Justice entirely fail to satisfy.

CONTENTS

CHAPTER I

THE SOCIAL AND SCIENTIFIC MOVEMENTS OF
THE TIME REGARDED FROM THE CHRISTIAN
POINT OF VIEW.

In studying some of the problems with
which the minds of men are occupied at the
present moment, I do not profess to take
up the position of an unbiassed inquirer.
I am convinced that Christianity helps us
more effectually than any other creed to
face and deal with these problems, and that
the new movements and demands which the
time is compelling us to study will help our
Christianity to become wider and deeper.
The task that I am attempting is to vin-
dicate the spiritual constitution of human
society, and to shew how order and progress
alike become more intelligible to us when
we invoke a Divine purpose to explain man

and the world. To consider the essential constitution of society is to come into close relations with inquiries in which almost all persons are now interested, with the discussions which are kindling the most heat, with the aims which are being prosecuted with the most eager enthusiasm. What is the nature of the ties which bind human beings together? What is the ultimate authority of the demands and restrictions which law and public opinion take upon them to enforce? What sort of ideal of human society is it legitimate or reasonable to keep before our minds? What hopes may we justly entertain with regard to the condition of the masses of mankind in the approaching future? These are questions to which men are earnestly seeking answers, and to which the Christian theory, as I shall contend, offers more enlightening and satisfying answers than can be obtained from any other philosophy.

It will be universally recognised that there are two movements, distinguishable from each other, which are equally characteristic of our time. The one is that of social and political exploration, the other that of scien-

tific discovery. The tide of each is felt to
be a resistless one, carrying us all with it.
Either the agitations of politics, or the
researches of science, with the novelty as
well as the importance which they may alike
undoubtedly claim to possess, may reasonably
excite and absorb a susceptible mind.

I. When we look at the course of
political movements in this country and the
other leading countries of the world, we see
that for many generations preceding our own
they have consisted in great part of the
struggles of non-privileged against privileged
classes, of the many against the few ; through
which struggles power has been gradually
obtained by the general body of the people.
Now that democracy is triumphant in the
sphere of legislation and government, it is
natural that the many, or those who interest
themselves on their behalf, should begin to
ask what the people, with their new powers,
can do for themselves. Some of the spokes-
men of democracy are showing a feverish
eagerness to spread all social advantages
immediately and by forcible methods over
the universal social surface. This could not
be said to be the temper of the genera

working-class population of this country: our people are for the most part sober enough, and slow to take up revolutionary schemes; but the idea that democratic government ought in some way to bring substantial advantage to the class which has the ultimate political power is undoubtedly permeating the popular mind. To get this desired improvement of the condition of the many accomplished, there must be more or less of change; there is sure to be some change—no one can pretend to foresee how much—in the laws relating to ownership, in the incidence of taxation, in the action and enterprise of the State. The prospect thus opened out is a stimulating one. It invites every poor man to hope that before long things may be made better, the chances may be rendered more favourable, for himself and his family. Some would say that the invitation is an appeal to individual covetousness; but the force of this covetousness,—if it were more reprehensible than any one can think it to be,—is weak compared with the force of the sympathy and philanthropy which the prospect awakens. The strength of socialistic agitation is not covetousness, but compassion for the poor. Who can be closely acquainted with the circumstances in which the poorest classes live, not only in crowded cities but in country districts also, without being moved by the current of this sympathy? Who would not be constrained to admit that almost any interference with the superior advantages of the well-to-do would be excusable, if it were certain that by such interference the miseries of extreme destitution might be banished from the land? The most ardent advocates of changes which are to benefit the poor are not those who suffer most from poverty themselves, but men to whose personal lot the changes for which they agitate would make little, if any, difference. I am not saying that all those who urge that something should be taken from the rich and given to the poor are animated by compassion only; but that this compassion is the primary and strongest force of their agitation. We are in presence of a popular movement which is partly in-spired by the Christian feeling of pity for the poor, which is sustained by the belief that the power of the many may rightly be used for the advantage of the many, and which is sure to make resolute efforts to improve by economical changes the relative position of the working classes, at the expense, if necessary, of their employers. This movement inevitably raises questions, not only as to possibilities and methods, but also as to rights and justice; and these questions, it is soon perceived, are by no means easy to answer.

II. We are in presence also of new scientific researches and conclusions, which happen to affect most closely the constitution of society. The science which is represented by the great names of Charles Darwin and Herbert Spencer undertakes to show that men have come to be in all respects what they are by natural and necessary processes of development. This doctrine confronts frigidly and firmly facts of history and life from which our Christianity—let it be admitted—would like to avert its eyes. It has one postulate, a universal animal craving for what is pleasant. Moved by this desire—so the science of evolution teaches — every animal tries to get as much as it can of what it likes. The early creature struggled for itself without caring what injury it might do to others. But animals found out by degrees how much individuals may gain by association. They may defend themselves more successfully by combining for defence; they may get more for each of what they all want by working together. Through this experience the whole complex organisation of society has grown into existence. Human beings now sacrifice themselves for others, because they are overmastered by a dominant habit, the product of countless generations of animal life, which has for its sole origin and sole reason the instinctive passion of self-love. This is the great paradox of the history of human nature as the theory of evolution reads it. Self-love works and works till it turns out to have generated self-sacrifice. All interpretations of life, the Christian amongst the rest, have paradoxes; this one, without caring whether it excites surprise or not, offers itself as simply registering the process of actual observed growth. The doctrine of evolution chiefly looks back, and describes growth as it has been. If it looks forward, it gives what may be described as a comforting forecast. It sees in the future the advantages of association commending themselves as much as ever to the individual mind; and it predicts, therefore, that there will be continued progress in the future along the lines of the past. But compassion, benevolence, sense of duty, forethought, hope, are forms of feeling under which this doctrine detects the single desire of what is agreeable to the individual, the struggle for a pleasant existence. In the eyes of the evolutionist philosophy all the ties of society, all the relations of human beings to each other, are natural products evolved out of the single original impulse or *nisus* of the universal creation.

There are some affinities between this latest science and socialistic democracy, but on the whole their voices are not in harmony. To quote from Häckel, one of the most advanced of the disciples of Darwin: "If a definite political tendency be attributed to Darwinism, this tendency can only be aristocratic, certainly not democratic, and least of all socialistic. The theory of selection teaches us that in human life, exactly as in animal and plant life, at each place and time only a small privileged minority can continue to exist and flourish; the great mass must

starve and more or less prematurely perish
in misery. . . . We may deeply mourn this
tragic fact, but we cannot deny or alter it.
'Many are called, but few are chosen!'"[1]
It might be urged, no doubt, in reply to this
judgment of Häckel's, that in human history
one great effect of evolution has been to
develop the habits of association, and so to
modify largely the simple competition of
individuals. But the ordinary assumptions
of socialistic democracy would be pronounced
by the naturalist philosopher to be sentimental
and fanciful; and Mr. Huxley has practised
his dialectical skill in tearing these assumptions to pieces.

This, however, the socialistic agitation
has in common with the theories of the
science of nature, that it confines its view
and its aims to this visible world. To some
of its leaders this world is all; they declare
that they see and know nothing above or
beyond it. Others are earnest Christians;
but, as social reformers, their professed aim
is to improve the material condition of the
many; and it satisfies their religious feeling

[1] Häckel, *Freie Wissenschaft und freie Lehre*, p. 73.

to know that the honouring of men as men, and care for the weak, are Christian principles, and that they are doing nothing inconsistent with their Christianity in asserting them and carrying them out.   It should be ungrudgingly recognised that some of those who are most enthusiastic in advocating economical changes in the interest of the many have in view better moral relations and a more truly human social life than the best which the present state of things as to rights and ownership allows, in their judgment, to be realised.   And all democratic reformers appeal with great confidence to justice as the support of their movement, though they are not able to say what justice is, or whence it derives its authority; and they may therefore be said to plant their lever in an unknown world.   But when these admissions have been made, it remains true that the social movement professedly and sometimes defiantly limits its scope to the visible world, and makes a more equal division of the good things of this life its primary object.

Is not this pursuit of material well-being —even the pursuit of it on behalf of others,

which must be allowed to be a different thing
morally from the pursuit of it for oneself—a
lower and poorer aim than that which makes
spiritual well-being its object? Is it capable
of waking up that which is noblest and best
in a man, of sustaining him against disappointment, of conquering inertia, of enlisting
the imagination, of kindling the purest and
most inextinguishable fire of the soul,—in
comparison with the contemplation of the
will of a perfect Creator, the consciousness of
being employed by him in accomplishing
his will in the world, the recognition of a
duty which urges from behind whilst the
divine glory attracts from before, the delight
of helping to make brother-men better
children of God and better members one of
another? Only one answer can rise within
us. It would seem hardly worth while to
put the question, but that there are persons
who, whilst they thrust aside with scorn all
that they call theology, will refer us triumph-
antly to marvellous examples of enthusiasm
and self-sacrifice in men and women who
with them know nothing of a God or a
Divine kingdom. To take the most tragical
of instances : we have been bidden to look at

the Russian revolutionists who have been
ready not only to die, but also—what often
requires much greater courage—to kill in
cold blood, for the sake of throwing their
country into a state of disorder out of which
a more equal distribution of the things of
this life, together with any contingent moral
results, may be won by the emancipated
masses. In Russia, undeniably, and in a
less striking degree in other countries, minds
have been set on flame and made capable of
any sacrifice by a passion for the removal
of outward restrictions and the material improvement of the condition of the many.
Whatever be the explanation of this zeal,
there is no ground for detracting from its
sincerity. But, for ourselves, we can judge
by our inward consciousness of the compara-
tive force of spiritual and temporal things on
our minds, for drawing out and nourishing
that which is best in them. A conviction or
hope or aim which descends from heaven to
lay hold of us will have more authority and
more inspiration for us than anything which
is only of earth can have.

However that may be, the Christian has

received, in that revelation or Gospel which makes him a Christian, a scheme of human existence which claims his reverent belief. To us Christians, man, whatever he may be to others, is a spiritual being, and human society a structure explained by its relations with an unseen world.   We hold ourselves to be creatures not of the earth or of nature, but of God; that is, of the incomprehensible Being who has made himself in some real manner, and in some adequate degree, knowable to us through Jesus Christ.   We are *in* this world, but not *of* it.   Looking back over past history we see, in the evolution of which science traces the method and stages, the working out of a spiritual purpose, the process of a spiritual discipline.   Before us shines an ideal, which we do not feel compelled to regard as created by our own imaginations, but which we believe to have been manifested to us as the Creator's design. We hold that each person is not even at liberty to do as he likes, still less that he is the necessary slave of impulses and desires which drive him; but that he has conduct prepared for him which he is bound by his relation to his Maker to follow, and that this conduct is suggested and defined by the relations in which he perceives himself to be placed towards his fellow-men. We hold, further, that it belongs to the spiritual training of mankind and of each man, that we should study these relations with reverence and interest, because they are living and growing products of the Creative Mind, and that thus we should find out from hour to hour, from age to age, what the conduct is which the relations demand. We look for hopeful and energetic effort on the part of men, in proportion as the glory of the future attracts their desires, and the good and acceptable and perfect will of the Maker reveals itself to them and makes them its willing instruments.

These, I think I may say, are the views of the Christian faith. I take it to be impossible for a convinced Christian not to bring these principles to bear, in his own mind, upon all the movements and conflicts and problems by which he is environed. That is to say, he has in his Christian belief the guiding principles of an ethical science and of a science of society. The statements I have just made are either elements of the simplest Christian faith or immediate deduc-

tions from it; and they are obviously funda-
mental in their nature, and have reference
both to the whole life of the individual man
and to the associated lives of men in society.
The Christian seems to have no alternative,
so long as he holds the belief of a Christian,
but to think of himself and of mankind in
accordance with those principles.

It has been generally assumed, however,
that Christians ought to have a theory or
science of ethics, and political and economic
views, independent of their religious creed.
Many of the leading writers on ethics and
the laws of society have been Christians ; but
in their treatises on these subjects they have,
for the most part, hardly allowed their
theological views to appear. Perhaps the
most real cause of this traditional exclusion
of theology from morals and politics has been
the fact that noble speculations on these
subjects, full of interest, richly instructive,
entitled by universal consent to be still
admired and studied, have come down to us
from pre-Christian times. Our students of
duty and society enter upon a field which was
long ago occupied by Plato and Aristotle and

the Stoics. Christian philosophers who have
upheld high and exacting principles of morality have been glad to claim for their
doctrines the support which they have found
in the *Ethics* of Aristotle or the *Republic* of
Plato, or the meditations of Epictetus and
Marcus Aurelius. They have shrunk from
beginning with assumptions which would
seem to make these venerated authorities of
no account. But they have had another
feeling also : they have regarded it as
important that they should take ground on
which they could meet philosophers of their
own time who are not ready to adopt the
Christian assumptions. They have feared
that there would be loss rather than gain, in
what concerns the higher life of the world,
if they should decline to know ethical and
political science except in the form of deduc-
tions from the Christian revelation. This
fear may well be stronger in the present day
than ever before. A Christian investigator
of moral and social questions can hardly help
saying to himself : " The followers of Mr.
Herbert Spencer will not look at anything I
may write if I make my conclusions depend
in any way on the Gospel of Christ. Such a

feature of an exposition would be enough to warn them off at once. The only chance of winning consideration in this field is to occupy common ground with rivals and opponents and allies to whom traditional Christianity is obsolete. It is open to a Christian to refer incidentally to Christ as the interesting author of the paradoxical precepts collected in the Sermon on the Mount; but he must take care not to assume that Christ and what has been revealed in him are to suggest and govern our speculations about history and duty."

I admit the weight of these considerations. Especially can I see it to be desirable in these days that as many as possible of those who—on whatever grounds—believe in a morality which has authority over men, and not merely in habits which grow out of men's likings, should stand side by side as supporters of a common cause. But I return to what appears to me incontrovertible. To a Christian's own mind, neither can human life, whether in the individual consciousness or in the societies of men, present itself apart from Christ; nor can Christianity present itself apart from the whole of human life. It is quite true that there are large branches of human knowledge to which it will make no apparent difference whether they are joined with or separated from Christianity and theology. The Gospel has no direct contact with mathematics, and it can hardly affect the conclusions of the mathematician—so far as the matter of his studies is concerned—whether or in what manner he believes in a God. If the New Testament be looked through, no allusion to the science of numbers will be found in it. But human life and motives are precisely what the Gospel of Christ claims for its own. If any one fancies for a moment that Christianity has no more than an arbitrary connection with conduct and economics and politics, he proves that the Christianity which he has in view is not the Christianity of Christ or the Apostles or Christendom.

It is a vital question for Christians, whether Christ is or is not a light enabling us to understand ourselves and the world better. It is not unreasonable that a man engaged in scientific investigation should resent the importing of arbitrary theological dogmas into what is a work of inquiry into facts. If Christianity presents itself to him as a system

of arbitrary theological dogmas, he will naturally regard it as an intruder, and claim that
he shall be allowed to co-ordinate his facts
and constitute his laws without reference to
it. But Christianity, in its original and
essential form of a Gospel concerning God
and his relations to men, professes to disclose
facts which without it would be hidden, to
explain to man the state in which he finds
himself and the feelings of which he is conscious, and to show him, through the dis-
closing of the spiritual environment and
foundations of his life, how he may rise into
a better state. To hold that the Gospel
treats men as individuals only, and has to do
with the solitary interests of the individual
conscience, and therefore that religion, from
the Christian point of view, is an affair of
each single man privately in relation to the
God in whom he has been induced to believe,
seems so complete and so wanton a misinter-
pretation of the New Testament and of the
history of Christendom, that it is difficult to
imagine how any one caring at all for Christianity could fall into such an error. It is
common enough for those who wish to keep
Christianity at arm's length to see it under

any perverted forms which may best suit
their purposes, and there are many persons
of various opinions who find it convenient to
assume that the law of Christ has no direct
authority over the public social life of men.
But that Christians, for the sake of avoiding
some troublesome problems, or of making all
religious societies self-governing and independent of the civil power, should be seduced
into adopting this maxim, would be incredible,
if there were not actual instances of it.

There could not be a more striking example of such seduction than that which is
to be found in a treatise [1] on Christianity and
Civil Society by the late Bishop Harris of
Michigan. The author, a man of whom the
American Church is justly proud, was an
enthusiastic citizen of the United States, to
whom the institutions of his country were
ideally perfect. This generous patriotism,
joined with a natural courage and thorough-
ness, led him to adopt the principle of the
separateness of Church and State with all its
consequences in its extremest form. He
held that God made the Church, and man

[1] *The Relation of Christianity to Civil Society:* the
Bohlen Lectures, 1882. New York, 1888.

made the State ; that man's highest relations
to God are those of an individual ; that individuals form themselves into societies, and
that the authority of civil society is derived
solely from the consent of the individuals who
compose it ; that the State will be the better
in its own non-spiritual sphere if the men
who associate themselves together are good
Christian men, and that civil life may thus be
affected by Christianity ; but that civil society
has nothing to do with God but through the
characters—humane and just, or otherwise—of
its constituent members.   It is impossible not
to admire the fearlessness with which Bishop
Harris maintained these principles.   Let me
quote a few sentences from his book.   " Here
are our two terms of relation,—a theocratic
Church which is wholly non-political, and a
social-compact State which is wholly secular.
The authority upon which the one rests is
the enactment and institution of a divine
founder.   The authority upon which the
other rests is the will of the people.   The
point of contact between the two is the
individual man " (p. 32).   The Gospel " completely changed the recognised basis of
authority in civil society. . . . The Church

was a pure theocracy, under which men were emancipated into the freedom, the dignity, the responsibility, of individuality. From this new standpoint civil society was seen to be wholly distinct from the Church, and to have no other basis than the consent of the people" (p. 58). The writer of the Declaration of Rights, "a devout communicant of the Church . . . had come to understand that the State is purely secular, while the Church is altogether spiritual ; that the State is altogether human, and the Church altogether divine" (p. 104). "The Church is theocratic, the State is democratic or popular. The State derives it real authority from beneath, the Church from above. The State is of this world, the Church is not of this world. . . . The object of the State is the maintenance of external order ; the object of the Church is the establishment of truth. The State has to do with those matters of expediency and propriety which are committed to it ; the Church has to do with the eternal things which concern the souls of men, and which each must face and deal with in his own personality" (p. 202). I should have thought that those to whom the stern

subjugation of the Southern States was the
great event of their lives must have lost faith
in the doctrine that the authority of civil
society rests entirely upon the consent of
those who make the social compact; and
that the religious fervour of the Civil War
would have forbidden to an American patriot
the language of Bishop Harris with regard
to the State and its basis and its province.
Could men kill and die by millions for
"matters of expediency and propriety"?

Churchmen who have to content themselves with the relations of Church and State in
the United States or the British Colonies are
in the same sort of position in which the good
Christians of a modern community find themselves with regard to general State schools.
These latter are compelled to acquiesce, either
in carefully generalised religious teaching
which they must regard as defective, or in a
completely secular education. But they do not
try to persuade themselves that either form
of instruction is ideally the best. The necessity of a compromise arises from the absence
of theological agreement amongst the members of a community. If all were of one
Church, it is certain that the doctrine of that

Church would be taught in the public schools;
and in the same case it is equally certain that
the Church would not be separate from the
State.   Where division exists, we have to
make the best of it ; and those who try to do
so will find, as in all actual states, that there
are some advantages in it, and that much
may be done to neutralise its disadvantages.

There are difficulties everywhere in holding and acting upon the belief that the one
Creator is the God of the State as well as of
the Church, the Ordainer of civil as well as
of ecclesiastical society.   But the God who
is known only as the God of the Church will
be a limited and private Divinity, very different in majesty and mystery of nature from
him whom we worship as the God of mankind.   And I think there can be no doubt
that the God to whom the Scriptures and the
Church Catholic bear witness is the Being
from whom all order, physical and human,
proceeds.   The Old Testament may be given
up by those whose God is the God of the
Church only, on the ground that Christ
revealed, as a new and revolutionary truth,
the earthliness of civil society.   But Gospels,
Epistles, Liturgies, Church History, all testify

against this imaginary revelation. The few sayings of Christ which have appeared to imply that the civil order and the kingdom of Christ are independent of each other may be shewn to have no such meaning. Let me briefly note them.

In answer to Pilate's question, "Art thou the king of the Jews?" our Lord said, " My kingdom is not of (or from) this world ; . . . is not from hence" (John xviii. 36). This is understood by some to imply that Christ's kingdom claims no authority over this world, has nothing to do with it. But that is not what Jesus said. He meant that his kingdom was from above, that it had not an earthly origin. So he had said to his Jewish enemies, "Ye are from beneath ; I am from above : ye are of this world ; I am not of this world " (John viii. 23). Yet Jesus had come into the world, as to his own property ; he had come to save the world. It is *because* Christ's kingdom is not from this world, not from beneath, but from above, that all the civil order in the world is to acknowledge him as its head. When he was asked about the payment of the tribute-money, Jesus enjoined, " Render to Caesar

the things that are Caesar's"; and he might
have stopped there.   No question had been
raised about ecclesiastical jurisdiction.   The
notion that our Lord would have claimed for
the Sanhedrim or the High Priest the homage
due to God is almost a ludicrous one.   But
the payment of tribute called up the thought
of rightful sovereignty.   And Jesus took occasion to drive home a reproach to the consciences of the hypocrites who were seeking
to ensnare him, by reminding them of the
Sovereign Lord to whom another kind of
tribute was due: "Render to God the
homage which is his due, that service of
heart and life which you know you are with-
holding from him; render your very selves
to God."   The claims of ecclesiastical, as dis-
tinguished from civil, authority, are entirely
foreign to this lesson.   Equally illegitimate
is it to build the doctrine which I am combat-
ing on our Lord's remonstrance, "Man, who
made me a judge or a divider over you?"
One out of the multitude had said to him,
"Master, bid my brother divide the inherit-
ance with me."   Jesus was angry at what he
perceived to be the attempt of a covetous
man to make use of him.   He openly stig-

matised the man as covetous by saying to
those who were present, " Take heed, and
keep yourselves from all covetousness." We
may almost assume that the man had tried
the ordinary law in vain, or knew that it
would not help him. Jesus repels the offen-
sive attempt by intimating to the offender
that he had come to the wrong quarter for
the prosecution of a pecuniary claim. To
infer from the indignant rebuff thus given
to an indecent covetousness that judges are
not to regard themselves as God's ministers,
but as only appointed "from beneath," is
more than unwarranted, it is almost contrary to what Christ implies. There is really
nothing in any saying of Christ or of his
Apostles to be set against the doctrine that
the civil order is directly of God, and that the
loyalty to be rendered to it is loyalty to God,
as implied in statements of this kind : " Thou
(Pilate) wouldest have no power (or authority)
against me, except it were given thee from
above " ; "there is no power (or authority)
but of God, and the powers that be are
ordained of God. . . . The ruler is a minister
of God to thee for good. . . . For this cause
ye pay tribute also, for they are ministers

of God's service." To distinguish between God's creation and man's creation, as Bishop Harris has done, is to fall into an error like that of our poet-recluse who wrote, "God made the country and man made the town." God made the town even more than he made the country, because man and his civilisation are higher works of God, and nearer to himself, than mountains and rivers and trees; and if God did not make the State more than he made the Church, he has made "the State," or the civil relations of human society, for countless millions for whom he has not yet made the Church.

It is superfluous to argue at any length that the Christianity of the New Testament expressly deals with man as a social being, and takes him as a whole. The Gospel addresses men as involved in all sorts of relations with their fellow-men, as constantly failing in the fulfilment of those relations, as not understanding them thoroughly, as having something perverse in their minds which rebels against them, as walking in a troublesome darkness and smitten with a harassing incapacity; in revealing Christ as their Friend and Head, and God as their

Father, it offers them an explanation of their condition, and a power to live in accordance with that which is appointed for them; and it presents to the imagination ideals which always imply harmonious and happy fulfilment of ordered mutual duties. How is it possible to leave any part of human life outside of such ideals? Man cannot know himself, and Christianity does not know him, except as a member of the social body to which he is related. The Gospel as declared by the Apostles called on men to wake up, to look around them, to accept the light which dawned and shone upon them, and to put all their strength with hopeful effort into the aim of conforming to the laws of which they were enabled now to see the reality and authority.

It seems to me, therefore, to be unreasonable that Christians should not prove their Christianity to the utmost in dealing with the problems of human life. To forbear to do so is like refusing a light that is offered you for exploring a dim and intricate limestone cave because there are others groping in it without a light. It is

a foolish as well as a disloyal policy to put
our Christianity behind us, and to beg our
non-Christian fellow-workers not to mind
it, for that it is really very innocent and
does not mean much, and will not be allowed
to be intrusive. If we are candid and
courageous, we shall acknowledge that we
have our Christianity on our hands, with all
its pretensions and claims, and that it must
submit to be tried by its power to do what
it professes that it was meant to do. If
there is truth in it,—if the Father of Jesus
Christ is really the Father of men, if Christ
is really the Light of the world,—I do not
say that Christianity will give us solutions
of all problems and answers to all questions,
and will save mankind the trouble of further
search and the discomfort of continued
ignorance and doubt : but not less than this
must be said, that it will guide us on the
right course ; that, if we let the Gospel teach
us, we shall be made aware of hidden realities
to which disordered appearances are pointing, and through relation to which those
appearances might be brought into harmony ;
that we shall be working and striving with
light from on high shedding sunbeams

around us, with light far in front of us drawing us continually onwards. We shall not be prevented from discussing duties with those who cannot tell why they are duties, if with us they acknowledge them to be duties ; or just relations with those who do not know why justice is binding on men, so long as they have some notion of what practical justice is, and feel its authority ; or freedom with those who are only acquainted with its lower forms but can honour as much as they see of it ; or good things, and ideals to be pursued, with those who can say no more than that they like them, if they are willing to like the things which are revealed to us as good and to desire the things which our God promises. We shall be in a rivalry with them, for which if we are right we have great advantages over them.

And while we shall want success to justify us in bringing our theology to bear upon social relations and duties, success — the power, I mean, to explain the actual world and to show the best way of dealing with it —will abundantly justify us. The world is before us, with its changing conditions. Never was there freer scope for all who

have either philosophies or remedies to try
upon the life of mankind. Words still have
power, but it is upon the condition that
effects shall follow them. " Thoughts are
but dreams," as Shakespeare has said, "till
their effects be tried." And it might not be
a bad thing if Christians were to lay aside
argumentative defence and assaults upon the
weak places of rival systems, and to resolve
to put their whole apologetic force into
practical guidance and construction. It
seems clear that such a course would be in
harmony with the original work of the
envoys of Christ in publishing the Gospel
and founding the Church. The aim of the
Apostles was to bring men out of darkness
into light, and to build up pure and happy
and progressive societies. And we, like
the Apostles, are worshippers of him who
shews to men that are in error the light of
his truth, to the intent that they may return
into the way of righteousness and may walk
happily therein. Our success will lie in
putting men into the right relations with
the things around them, in suggesting to
them how they may conquer the hindrances
which confuse and weaken them, and in

helping them to walk with hope as those who see their way and the goal towards which they are tending. The goal, indeed, best defines the way : " Lord," said Thomas to his Master, " we know not whither Thou goest : how know we the way ? " They who see a goal, however dimly, before them, will understand that they have to walk directly towards it, helping and cheering one another amidst the difficulties and wearinesses of the way. That was a significant title, indeed,—the Way,—that was given to their religion by the first Christians. Saul, if he found any " of the way " at Damascus, was to bring them bound to Jerusalem. It was an abbreviated form of several equivalent phrases, by which Christianity was described. " These men . . . proclaim unto you the way of salvation." Apollos " had been instructed in the way of the Lord." But it was a fine instinct that felt that the new religion might characteristically be named by this one word : it recognised that Christians were to regard themselves as called to walk in a certain way towards a goal which was shewn to them.

I am to ask my readers, then, to look

frankly upon human society as not explained
or fully accounted for by what is visible and
earthly, but as having a spiritual constitution,
an unseen Lord, a spiritual life to lead, a
spiritual destiny to fulfil. It may be that in
such contemplations we shall be in some
degree dissociating ourselves from those who
have only known Christianity as a scheme
for rescuing individuals out of a perishing
world and endowing them with perpetual
happiness in the world beyond the grave.
But any one who passes from that conception
of Christianity to such a one as we are
assuming will find, it may be confidently
said, a new light shining upon the sacred
books of our faith. The Gospels, he will
see, are setting forth a kingdom of heaven,
which was heralded by John the Baptist, had
been foreshadowed by the national prophets
of Israel, and was brought in by the Son of
God; and which was to grow in the world
till the world should be covered by it and
made its own. He will find St. Paul occupied
with continual thoughts of the binding of
men together in Christ, of marvellous dis-
closures of Divine purpose in the handling
and training of mankind, of developments of

redeeming and constructive action which age
after age was to work out and exhibit.   There
is no book of the New Testament which is
not more concerned with social and progressive Christian life than with the felicity of
individuals in escaping from the pains and
securing the pleasures of the future world.

Looking at mankind thus, from the point
of view of the New Testament, we ought, I
take it, to be greatly interested by the agitations, speculations, and demands which the
progress of democracy is everywhere stimulating.   There may be serious economic
errors in the schemes which attract the
ardent friends and champions of the poorer
classes ; it seems almost obvious, indeed, that
the short cuts to universal comfort to be
made by means of the legislative manipula-
tion of property are delusive ways : and it is
very desirable that losses and disappointments
should be prevented by the diffusion of
economic knowledge, so that the unsparing
correction of experience may not be needed
to impart wisdom to communities refusing to
be otherwise taught.   But the believer in
the kingdom of heaven can never have

reconciled himself to the physical disadvantages from which the life of the poor suffers
in comparison with that of the rich, nor to
the moral disadvantages which make it
especially difficult for the rich to enter into
that kingdom : and he must recognise
Christian hopes and ideas in much of what
is stirring the hearts and imaginations of
those who make up the masses. What he
will observe with misgivings is the general
agreement to look to material equality and
material comfort as the supreme objects.
Equality has no real title to be a serious
object of pursuit; neither Nature nor the
Gospel pays it any homage. And it is
certain that the teaching of Christ is one
continued warning against the setting of the
heart on the things of this life as the true
treasures. It cannot be admitted that in the
light of the Gospel the poor man is any more
justified than the rich man in making the
things which money can buy his principal
consideration.

And what will be our attitude towards
that haughty science of which evolution is at
once the creed and the divinity, which sees
in all human affections only so many dis-

guises of the primary animal craving?—
Within its own region of natural history, in
its own business of the tracing of processes,
we cannot but pay deference to its claims
and its conclusions. We shall feel bound to
refrain from outcries as we see it, however
untenderly, correcting errors into which
religion has fallen. We ought to have faith
to welcome with admiration and thankfulness
all that it discovers, as so much revelation of
the creative methods of the God whom we
worship. But we shall insist on its being
noted that, if evolution is all, if all that a man
can know is that he and other things have
come to be what they are by processes of
cause and effect which could not have been
otherwise, then the qualities which we have
been taught and are resolved to prize most
in human life are smitten with blindness and
death. Where is the place for reverence,
where for hope, where for thankfulness,
where for purpose and choice, where for
faith, where for self-offering, where—might
we not ask—for love itself, if the only real
knowledge is the perception of the necessary
successions of nature? Let us allow fully
what naturalist science can do: it may breed

wonder, it may feed the intelligence, it may cultivate accuracy of statement and modesty of pretension ; but, if it claims to be all knowledge, it smiles at the sense of duty, at delight in serving, at the trustful hope that rises superior to every disappointment, as illusions which the instructed eye can see through. We do not claim for spiritual affections, such as we name conscience, and reverence, and gratitude, and hope, and resolution, and devotion, that they have a right to create a God and a heaven and an ideal world to which they may attach themselves. But we cannot help honouring them as witnesses ; and we hear them bearing witness to what has been revealed to us in Christ. And we hold it reasonable to believe that any doctrine which commends itself to these affections and causes them to grow in their beneficent health, has therein the best confirmation that our minds are able to receive.

CHAPTER II

THE IDEAL UNITY OF MANKIND IN THE UNIVERSAL CHURCH

In discussing the ties which bind men together, it is often neither necessary nor desirable to extend our view far beyond the circle of those with whom we are ourselves connected. But we find ourselves easily drawn on from the narrower to the wider circles; and we cannot consider what most deeply concerns man without being constrained to think of all mankind. This larger view is more habitual to speculators in these days than it has been previously, for two chief reasons:—we now embrace the whole world with some sort of knowledge, and are at least roughly acquainted with the populations to be found in any part of it; and we of this generation have also a greatly increased knowledge of the past history of the human

race as a whole. Our students of the primitive history of man have for some time been
guided by the luminous principle that the
present condition of the most backward races
resembles the prehistoric condition of the
races which are now the most civilised. The
application of this principle is beset by some
difficulties and obstacles like those which
delay the inquirers who investigate the
history of life upon this globe; but on the
whole the great fact of gradual development
and progress asserts itself increasingly and
irresistibly. We are accustoming ourselves,
not very willingly, to think of the races of
men as having been slowly and unequally
civilised, rising from stages even lower than
that of the least civilised population which
travellers have described to what they
respectively are now. It must be admitted
that this view disturbs greatly the traditional
Christian conceptions of human history : we
cannot yet determine in what respects and to
what lengths it will ultimately modify them.
But when the faith in Christ and the Father
has proved its power to assimilate the new
scientific doctrine, it will be seen to have
achieved a greater triumph, and to have

entitled itself to a higher authority over the minds of men, than it has won in any previous religious crisis. I cannot understand how any Christian mind can fail to be somewhat troubled by those savage populations living in animal habits through æons of æons. It is not easy to fit the existing uncivilised tribes, some of which seem destined not to be a practical difficulty to us much longer, into any scheme of the government of mankind by a gracious Father; but there is something yet more oppressive, and more difficult to adjust to the biblical traditions, in that aspect of the past which anthropology presents to our view.

It cannot be said that the actual origin of mankind is yet made clear to us. The gap between man and the ape is not completely bridged over so as to connect the lowest known man either with the highest known ape amongst the present tenants of the earth, or with any which the remains preserved by the earth under its surface have disclosed to us. Many avenues of thought and discovery end for us in baffling obscurity. We find ourselves encouraged to push our speculations and researches as far as we can; but there is always a point at which the Maker says to us, Thus far shalt thou go, and no farther. It is intended, we must conclude, that we shall derive our chief and most trustworthy knowledge from what we can see around us, from what we can study in the actual play of mutual relations. Something of the past is brought under our view, that we may know change and progress and development; and something of the future is presented to our imagination, that we may be drawn onward by it. We are made conscious that we are limited and dependent creatures, able to know that there are things we cannot know, checked to our unavailing surprise and impatience by insoluble questions and unaccountable contradictions. There is no higher wisdom for us than to take hold humbly of the Hand held out to guide us.

If we look around us over the world with the thought of the constitution of society in our minds, it will be natural that we should first take note of the existence of Christendom. There are a number of nations and races which are united by the common pro-

fession of the Christian religion. These are
the principal races and nations of the world.
Christendom embraces all Europe, both the
Americas, considerable portions of Asia and
Africa. The Christian faith has been heredi-
tary for many generations in Europe, and its
extension over other parts of the globe has
been due more largely to migration of European races than to the propagation of the
faith amongst non-Christians. But Christianity began in Asia ; salvation was from the
Jews. The proclamation of a crucified Jew
as the Son of God, and of the kingdom in
which he ruled as divine and universal, was
accepted by gradually increasing numbers in
the course of many ages, until every European people submitted to the Christ as Lord.
The Christian religion, thus widely dominant,
brings to our minds other religions. Facing
the religion of the New Testament along a
border of some length stands the religion of
the Koran, founded similarly within historic
times, and propagated also similarly over a
wide area from an obscure Eastern centre.
The third of the great religions of the world
is the Buddhist, the beginnings of which are
not so well known as those of the other two,

but are not out of the reach of investigation.
There is a medley of other religions, descend-
ing to a chaos of almost incredible supersti-
tions.   It is alleged that tribes have been
found having no religion at all ; but if this is
true, they comprise an insignificant portion
of the human race.   As a rule, human beings
living together have always had some beliefs
in supernatural powers, and these beliefs have
exercised a more controlling influence than
any others over their lives.   Some philosophers hold that they can trace religion to its
very first roots in the natural delusions of the
most undeveloped of mankind, and can show
with precision by what necessary processes it
has undergone its innumerable modifications.

Of the religion which is professed by
Christendom, and which has had so much
to do with the progress of mankind, it is a
special characteristic that it claims to be
intended for the whole world.   The same
pretension may, no doubt, be put forth on
behalf of Islam and Buddhism ; but the
character of a Universal Religion is more
conspicuous in Christianity and has been
more persistently asserted by its advocates.
We speak for convenience' sake of Christian-

ity as a religion, but this name was not used by its founders. They spoke, instead, of a Gospel and a Church. They described themselves as envoys, charged with a message of forgiveness and promise from the God of heaven and earth; and their work was to found in every place societies of those who received their word as authentic and accepted Jesus the Crucified as their Divine Lord. A religion was, no doubt, a result of the preaching of the Apostles; that is to say, a combination of creed and worship,—statements of what was held with regard to the supernatural world by believers in Christ and the Father, joined with common modes in which they offered their prayers and their praise. But when Christians have regarded themselves as the adherents of a religion, they have always been weaker than when they reckoned themselves as having received a Gospel and as forming a Church. To substitute the Christian religion for the Gospel of Christ and the Catholic Church has been as injurious to Christianity as it has been plainly a departure from the methods of its founders. All Christians are properly, not professors of a religion, but members of the Catholic

Church. Those who commend Christianity as the best of the religions of the world, but pronounce it to be good for certain races only and deprecate its being pressed upon other races, are superior persons not really sharing the beliefs on which they look down with indulgence. It is not easy to imagine what a local Christianity, intelligently held, could be. If it regards Christ as divine, it must claim the whole world for Him ; if it does not, it must reject nearly all the traditional creeds and prayers of the Church, and must go on purging itself till it ceases to be Christianity, and becomes a residuum of sentiment and morality to which other religions ought, on its principles, similarly to reduce themselves. A religion true and good for one race cannot well help being the proper religion for all races.

It would seem that the name Catholic, when it was first joined to Church by the sub-Apostolic Christians, meant the united body of all the local churches, and was hardly intended to imply of itself that the Church of Christ aimed at embracing all mankind. But perhaps the former sense passes naturally into the latter. Certainly, when we look at the

Christian communities as they are now spread over the face of the globe, and think of the Catholic Church as the body comprehending these, we cannot help receiving at the same time the impression that the Church opens its doors to all mankind, and, according to the glorious traditions of its whole history, claims all peoples and tongues for its own. When once the barrier between Jew and Gentile was broken down under the ministry of the Apostles, the universality of the Church in its fullest sense was established. For the Jew, believing in the election and separateness of his own nation, knew of no distinctions amongst the Gentiles, and the fusion of Jew and Gentile in the Christian society implied the freest and amplest admission into that society of Greek and Roman, barbarian and Scythian, Indian and Chinese alike.

But when we look at the Christendom around us more closely, what we see is no united Christian society bound together by the same creed and common usages of worship and a single system of government; but a multitude of societies, all calling themselves Christian, each drawing a certain cincture round itself by distinctions of belief and ritual and government, all regarding each other with more or less of disapproval. The observer cannot but ask himself, " Where is the Catholic Church ? is it broken into these fragments, and itself lost from the world ? Or are we to speak of it as still existing ? If so, what is it ? " That is a question which has been exercising the minds of very many Christians in England during the last three-quarters of a century. All the secessions to the Church of Rome that have taken place in that time have been due to the belief that the Papal Church is the Catholic Church. " The Catholic Church must be somewhere upon the earth," it has been argued, " if Christianity is still to be regarded as true. It must have unity for its most obvious feature. You cannot take bodies which excommunicate each other, two or three or any number, and say that these form together a single society which can be named the One Catholic and Apostolic Church. There is one society in these days which claims to be by itself and exclusively the Catholic Church, and that is the society which historically has the best title to represent the original undivided Christendom."

In vindicating the spiritual constitution of human society, I desire to maintain that the Catholic Church, rightly understood, is the form of the appointed union and communion of mankind. The question, How is the Catholic Church to be understood? is therefore one which directly concerns our subject. Let us look at this question from the point of view of members of the Church of England.

It must be admitted that the Anglican position is an anomalous one, of which it is not easy to give a good logical justification. It is none the less likely on this account to be a good position, made for us by the God of history instead of being chosen by ourselves or by our fathers, having peculiar advantages which it is our duty to study and develop and use. It must be a deep and obstinate feeling that this is so, such a real faith in God's guiding providence as is wiser than logical satisfaction, that has kept Anglicans in general from following the lead of those who have sought a home in the Papal Church. We know what can be said in defence of our separation from that Church. We claim that we retained at the Reformation, and still retain, all the links of historical con-

nection with the original Catholic Church,
and that submission to the Bishop of Rome
is not one of such links. We charge the
Roman Church with being in fault, and with
being to such a degree in fault as to be
responsible for the schism. We charge that
Church with having gradually adopted doctrines and practices which were unknown to
the primitive Catholic Church,—corruptions
which those who desire to be loyal to primitive Christianity might perhaps tolerate in
others rather than separate openly from them,
but which they cannot accept, when it is
sought to impose them by authority, as
parts of their own religion. We may regard
our renunciation of the Papal claims as a
provisional and temporary protest, only prolonged—though it be prolonged for centuries
—until it please God to bring the authorities
of the Roman Church to a better mind, and
so to make reunion possible. We derive
some comfort from the contemplation of the
Greek Church and other Eastern Churches,
which shew us that we do not stand alone in
our separation from Rome, but that there are
other Christian bodies not acknowledging the
authority of the Pope which have as good a

claim as the Church of Rome, on the grounds of historical continuity and loyalty to primitive Catholicity, to be regarded as portions of the Catholic Church. But to a mind possessed by the idea of a visible and perpetual Society founded and organised by Christ, and endowed with his own authority, the See of Rome, with its unbroken traditions, its ancient territory, its wide rule, its assumption of universal dominion,—not to speak of its spiritual graces, which there is a good deal of an opposite character to neutralise,—must have an imposing authority and a reasonable fascination ; whilst the position of the Church of England, after the best that can be said for it from the Catholic point of view, must remain disturbingly irregular and unsatisfactory.

It has become a sort of tradition with Englishmen to acquiesce in anomalies, and even to be rather proud of them ; and it is a sound faith, having much support in our experience, that irregularities of the surface and the absence of logical cohesion may be signs of an increasing Purpose running through the ages, and may point to a unity deeper than that of external order. Holding fast this faith, let us note without shrinking how we stand. The Anglican Churches form now a great communion, and an assemblage of their bishops is no inconsiderable Council. The English Church may say with the Patriarch, "With my staff I passed over this Jordan, and now I am become two bands." At the time when it put its Jordan between the See of Rome and itself, it had for its people the scanty population of this island, drawn rather by loyalty to the sovereign than by religious conviction. Rome claimed the submission of the king or the queen as well as of the clergy, and the revolt against the Pope was a royal and national act, which carried the clergy with it. The civil power, essentially national under the Tudor rule, took to itself a large part, not at any moment strictly defined, of the ecclesiastical authority which it wrested from Rome. We have in England no corporate society consisting of members of the Church. There is no such person as a member of the Church of England known by any definition to our law. The Church, as such, has no self-government. There is an ecclesiastical organisation, all the parts of which are recognised and supported by the

law of the land.   We have bishops and dio-
ceses, parsons and parishes ; bishops, priests,
and deacons ; churches and a ritual and
churchwardens ; two clerical assemblies, one
for each archiepiscopal province ; possessions
belonging to ecclesiastical bodies and persons,
and a central Commission, appointed by the
civil power, exercising an important control
over these possessions.   The law of the
Reformation period assumed that in England
every one subject to the law belonged also to
the Church ; and the assumption has only
been modified in the way of exempting from
certain ecclesiastical obligations those who
like to claim the exemption.   The Church
in England has for the most part been
thought of as the ecclesiastical organisation
of the land sustained and controlled by the
national authorities ; and this Church has
had for its people or members all English
subjects who have not expressly dissociated
themselves from it.   There are many at this
time, clergymen and laymen, who cling to a
tradition of a certain constitutional co-ordinate
power in the Convocations over matters of
doctrine and ritual ; but whilst there are
those who declare that they will submit to

no change in these matters which is not sanctioned by a Convocation, no one has yet been found who undertakes to submit to a decree of a Convocation, whatever it may be, as of itself binding upon him. There is indeed no existing authority, or combination of authorities, to which all clergymen hold themselves bound to submit; which is a peculiar and inconvenient feature of the present condition of the Church in this country.

Must it not be allowed, then, that we English Churchmen, whose first business is with our own case, stand in a curiously dislocated relation towards the presumed universal Church or society of Christ? When we look beyond ourselves, besides those Churches which in common with English Churchmen make much of historic continuity and succession, and especially as regards the order of bishops, we have before our eyes the Christian communities which have broken off, not only from Rome, but from the tradition of the early Church, and which have no bishops at all, or none who claim direct descent from the Apostles. These communities are so large and im-

portant, they have so much of real devotion
to Christ, they manifest the graces of
Christian life so abundantly and attractively,
they are so hearty and so rational in their
allegiance to the sacred volume accepted by
all Christendom, that it is utterly impossible,
in considering Christendom, to leave them
out of account. Those who feel bound to
excommunicate these bodies for their want
of Episcopacy cannot bring themselves to
disown the members of them as fellow-members of Christ. But what a Christendom
it is that we look out upon, we English
Christians, when we desire to see that Holy
Catholic Church in which we believe!
Christianity, indeed, we see more widely
extended over the globe than ever: but
where is the one Society of the first days?
It was not the baseless fabric of a vision,
because it has left so many wracks behind:
but must we not conclude in despair that it
was one of the failures of poor humanity?
Whilst it was still very small, it was a real
society, and it had the Divine ambition of
drawing all men as fellow-members into
itself. But what was practicable on the
small scale was not, it appears, practicable

on a large scale ; the organism grew, but it
began to crack and split, and it is now
broken up into a number of fragments,
severally by no means unworthy of consideration and respect—but fragments ; and
not only without cohesion, but actually
hustling each other, and almost in a state of
war.

If, however, we go back to St. Paul, the
greatest of the founders of the Church, and
the thinker from whom our chief conceptions
and phrases about the Church are derived,
we shall find reasons for believing that he
would warn us against such despair and
would bid us take courage. For the Church,
in his pages, is plainly not the mere aggregate of the societies which he and the
Twelve had created. The Church of St.
Paul's Epistles is an ideal body ; and the
Christian societies of his day were far from
being ideally perfect. Some modern inter-
preters of the Apostolic records, going beyond
the things which are written, would have us
believe that amongst the Twelve, even, there
were deadly jealousies, and that between
Paul and the leaders of the Twelve there
was violent opposition and untempered de-

nunciation. We need not think thus of these elect souls, these loyal servants of the one Master; but we must admit that the differences thus exaggerated were in reality such as to cause pain and some scandal, and that the leaders who themselves held together in Christ had followers who acted as vulgar partisans. To St. Paul the Church was an ideal body, of which Christ was the head, and Christians as they should be— societies and individuals—the limbs and organs. He would not look at them only as they were,—members of the same local Church often separated from each other by private quarrels and factious partisanship, sometimes a whole Church, as at Corinth, rebelling for a time against its founder. It may not be quite easy for us to put ourselves at his point of view. We must be able to distinguish between an ideal and an imaginary body. If a non-Christian had assumed that this Jew's idea of a Church was nothing but a creature of his imagination, St. Paul would have taken the assumption as a matter of course : but he would have been impatient if a fellow-Christian had regarded the idea of Christ's body as anything but most real.

The Church was the creature of God's purpose, the design which God was working out in the history of mankind. The visible embodiment, in the actual Christian society, was not separate from the Divine idea, nor was the Divine idea separate from the visible embodiment. The Christian societies could not have been what they were, in fellowship and hope and conquest of the world, had not God been moulding them after his perfect system, and quickening them with his perfect life; and the pattern was, Christ the Head and men the members, all the members performing their several functions in happiness and harmony; and the life, the one Spirit of the Father and the Son. And this invisible work of God could not have been thought of as real, unless it had been clothing itself with the actual history of human beings. But the Divine idea, instinct with the living Divine energy, did not bring its work summarily to perfection. It was content with gradual growth, it could bear with defects and faults; and these shortcomings were manifold and grievous in every association of believers. God's will and design for every member was that he should be in such healthy attachment and subordination to the Head, so tied by spiritual nerves and muscles to his fellow-members, that the body might be an irreproachable and efficient body. The Church figured itself to the Apostolic eye as a glorious bride, not having spot or wrinkle or any such thing; the human society thus figured was called to be holy and without blemish. And towards this perfection the Divine energy was continually striving. But it did not overpower the rebellion or the inertia of human wills. "Not holding fast the Head," οὐ κρατῶν τὴν κεφαλήν, was the account which St. Paul had to give of many a Christian, in some degree of every Christian. If only each had been able to hold fast the Head, the perfect Divine idea would have had a less imperfect historical clothing. But even as it was, any one looking at what was proper and distinctive in the Christian societies, at what was good and constructive and productive in them, was in the way to discern the body, and to perceive it to be Christ's.

There seems to be no reason why we in this age should have a different conception of the Church Catholic from that which St.

Paul had.   If we take his view, the Church
Catholic, the universal Church, is first invisible, and secondarily visible; not in the
sense in which the distinction has been used
in modern times by those who make the invisible Church consist of a certain number of
visible persons whom Christ sees to be alone
his true members amongst the multitude of
apparent Christians; but invisible, as the
mystical or ideal Society which is the inner
creative substance of the earthly Christian
societies, the perfect structure up to which
they all are growing; and visible, as being
represented in these human societies, which
are made up of the very mixed materials of
human nature, are far from being ideally
perfect in knowledge or in life, but are
struggling forward, and all doing something
to make the one Catholic Church an outward
existence in the world.   If, in obedience to
the Christian impulse which prompts us to
look for good in all things, we try to find
some comforting explanation of the divisions
of Christendom, it is possible to perceive that
they are turned to good account in two ways:
they effectually hinder Christians from sub-
stituting the seen for the unseen, the body

for the Head,—a fatal evil into which a well-compacted earthly Catholic Church might betray them ; and, through the various forms which Christianity has taken and the different lines along which it has pushed its energies, these divisions which trouble us may have been made the means of giving a fuller presentation of the Divine idea than a single Church would have been able, or at least likely, to exhibit.

Have orthodox Churchmen ever clearly recognised what a justification of irregularity is to be found in the commission and work of the Apostle Paul ? Nothing could be more definite than the authority given to the Twelve. The special admission of St. Matthias, in the place of the Traitor, was intended to preserve the outward completeness of that authority. The Twelve were to sit on twelve thrones. They actually ruled the Church as its authorised official chiefs during its early years. But Saul of Tarsus arose, claiming that a special commission had been given to him in visions. The regular course would have been that he should have submitted his pretensions and credentials to the Twelve, and that they, if they thought

fit, should have sent him forth. But he did
not ask them to sanction his work. He
maintained an almost ostentatious independence. He acted on the assumption that the
commission given to him in visions was as
good as that which the Twelve had received.
His Master was the Master of the Twelve,
and Paul professed an earnest desire to work
in harmony with them ; but the co-operation
was to be on terms of equality. With a
certain haughtiness St. Paul was accustomed
to declare that he would produce no credentials except the results which he accomplished,
the Churches which he founded. His pretensions were abundantly, irresistibly justified;
but it was at the cost of formal regularity.

Instead therefore of regarding the many
Churches of Christendom as the fragments
which show that the Catholic Church has
been broken to pieces, as the ruins of the one
Temple of God, of the one City of God, we
shall see in their variety a proof that the
Catholic Church which each of them aims at
representing is something more comprehensive and more spiritual than the best of them.
They may encourage us as prophecies of a
greater unity yet to be realised, instead of

depressing us as memorials of a unity that has been lost. Members of each religious communion, if they are thus advised, may go on repeating more earnestly than ever their belief in the Holy Catholic Church as the hidden spiritual structure which binds them all together, and which has in each a more or less inadequate expression. And the way to the more glorious unity of the future will be not so much through attempts to create a complete and exclusive Church by mutual concessions and compromises, but through a growing loyalty of each believer and each body of believers to the unseen Head. We may leave in God's hands the work of building up universal mankind into the universal Church of his Son, that he may accomplish it in his own manner and his own time, bending ourselves for our part to the fulfilment of the clear duty of endeavouring to keep the unity of the Spirit in obedience to Christ. We of the English Church shall justify with a clear conscience our traditional tolerance of anomalies, so long as they do not choke spiritual life ; and shall be careful not to cast away, in the craving for outward regularity, any historical element which may

be the means of enabling us to perform more
effectively our appointed share of the great
Divine operation.

If, with the faith of Catholic Christians,
we believe in Christ as the Head of all mankind, it will be impossible that we should not
see in this relation the most comprehensive
and the most authoritative of human bonds.
It is in the Church Catholic—that is, in the
whole human race acknowledging its true
Head—that the proper unity of mankind
consists and is explained. This unity is
always getting itself confessed by all men,
whatever their faith may be. That men are
in some way bound together, that to any man
nothing that is human is altogether alien, is
a creed which nature teaches, and which
forms the ground of all good and humane
effort. It is one of the chief lessons set to
this generation, to learn the brotherly obligations of nation to nation, of the civilised to
the uncivilised, of all men to all men. The
worshipper of evolution will see in this comprehensive humanity only a wider extension
of those tribal feelings and habits which grow
out of the discovery that each man is stronger
and happier when he joins himself with others

than when he stands alone. The course of things, the evolutionist observes, is teaching men that a nation had better not be quarrelsome in dealing with other nations, any more than clansman with clansman. The growth of international sympathies, he holds, will by degrees make the strong civilised race dislike taking advantage of the weak and uncivilised. Others, whilst they recognise no headship of mankind, will yet use and feel warranted in using the language of obligation, will speak of right and wrong as well as of evolved feelings, with regard to the action of the strong towards the weak. They find in themselves an acknowledgment of what is right and best in relations and behaviour, there are ideas of justice and of duty and of mutual regard in the air which speak to them with authority, and the dictates of which are confirmed by contemplation and experience ; and they will not only act upon these themselves, but they will peremptorily call on fellow-men to act upon them also. They will maintain that it is a shame for the strong to oppress the weak, for the knowing to circumvent the simple, in Africa or in Asia as well as in England or the United States. And there is no known worshipper of evolution who does not allow himself to be drawn beyond the range of his proper observations into the admissions and appeals of those who thus worship the ideas of righteousness and love. The Catholic Christian goes the whole length of their roads both with the worshipper of evolution and with the worshipper of moral ideas. He recognises with devout reverence that the Father of men is leading mankind by the evolutionary processes of his providence into the ways of universal concord. The ideas of justice and goodwill, of reciprocal obligations, of the embracing of every human being within the bonds of humanity, are to him also in the air. They are not only in the air, because he knows how they come there and understands the authority which they claim; and he adores them as the attributes of the Father who has exalted the Divine Son of man to be the Head of his body the Church; but they *are* in the air, being the very Breath of God, what the Christian names the Spirit of the Father and the Son, of which we have all been made to drink. Whoever confesses the authority of righteousness and love must

needs be thought of by the Catholic Christian
as a fellow-worshipper of his God.

There are certain problems,—speculative
problems, for example, as to the unity of
origin of the races of mankind, and as to the
distinctions between man and the inferior
animal races, and practical problems as to the
reasonable rights of the lower human races
and the best treatment of them, and as to the
possibility of combining all sorts of races in
one creed—which present difficulties to us
all alike, but which cause, it may be admitted,
more anxiety and pain to Christian thinkers
than to others. The claim to see by a light
in the heavens which other men do not use
has its responsibilities and its inconveniences.
If the Purpose of. God revealed in Christ
sheds illumination over our spiritual nature
and the world to which it belongs, it makes
the dark places of creation and history more
incomprehensible. When we have reasoned
our utmost about some of the difficulties
which try the faith of the Christian, there
may be nothing for us to do but to leave off
reasoning, to admit the difficulties with can-
dour, and to pass on. We may gather, I
repeat, from these experiences of our help-

lessness that we are intended to see a little way backwards into the past, that we may understand our surroundings and ourselves the better; a little way before us into the future, that the glory of it may attract us: but chiefly to look around us into our own environment, and upwards to the heaven above.

There are two great subjects, Trade and War, which are especially demanding the attention and exciting the interest of those who recognise the brotherly bond uniting all men and all races of men together. On the principles of trade Catholic Christianity has anticipated political economy. Before this modern science was born or thought of, the meaning of trade was thus expounded by Christian faith[1]: "Forasmuch as the great and Almighty God hath given unto mankind, above all other living creatures, such an heart and desire, that every man desireth to join friendship with other, to love and be loved, also to give and receive mutual benefits: it is therefore the duty of all men according

---

[1] From Letters Missive of Edward VI., A.D. 1553, preserved in Hackluyt, and in Harris's *Voyages and Travels*, 1705, vol. i. p. 507.

to their power to maintain and increase this
desire in every man, with well-deserving to
all men, and especially to show this good
affection to such as being moved with this
desire come to them from far countries. . . .
For the God of heaven and earth, greatly
providing for mankind, would not that all
things should be found in one region, to the
end that one should have need of another,
that by this means friendship might be
established among all men, and every one
seek to gratify all." The Christianity of the
type illustrated in these noble sentences of
some minister of Edward VI. is evidently in
favour of the utmost freedom of trade. The
democratic spirit of our day, whilst it would
be greatly attracted by these sentiments, is
embarrassed as to adopting them and carrying
them out, partly by want of economic knowledge, partly by national prepossessions.
Those who would call themselves Socialists
are very much inclined to be cosmopolitan,
and one of their dreams is of such a combination of the working-classes of the world as
would enable them to dictate their own terms
to capitalists of all nations ; but, on the other
hand, the working people of each country

regard foreign competition as directly injurious to their interests, and a superficial view
of the influences affecting their condition is
apt to make them favourable to the protection
of native industries, and to the exclusion of
foreign labour and foreign products. Considering that the democratic population of
every other country in the world, including
our own colonies, is insisting upon a policy
of protection, or what has been called
nationalist economy, it ought not to surprise
us if the working classes here in England,
when they realise that by putting forth their
combined strength they can sway the government of the country, should aim at making
their respective trades more prosperous by
putting checks on foreign competition.
Christianity should throw the weight of its
consciousness of the common humanity and
its sense of the sacredness of the ties which
bind all men and all nations together against
any action of separate countries which would
be detrimental to the general prosperity of
the world. Those who believe with our
forefathers in a God of heaven and earth
greatly providing for mankind, will be slow
to believe that nations can be benefited in

the long run by a policy of self-protecting exclusiveness.

That it is right, however, for a nation to defend itself all Christians, except the followers of George Fox, have allowed ; and we have to face the paradox that war is not forbidden by the religion which declares all men to be brothers. Certainly there must be something wrong when brothers have to do their best to kill and impoverish brothers. But the duty of fighting in certain circumstances is a witness that there are better things to care for than physical life and freedom from physical pain. The independence and honour of a nation, the repression of wrong-doing and insolence, are objects in behalf of which it is not merely legitimate, but a duty to God and to mankind, to come to blows. God, let us not hesitate to say, teaches hands to war and fingers to fight for the defence of the order of the world against those who would violate it. The Father of all men hates ill-will and deceit more than wounds and death ; and it would be quite possible to hate more and deceive more in submitting to an aggressor than in meeting him on the field of battle. The feelings of soldiers arrayed against each

other, even in the heat of conflict, are not
necessarily as murderous as their acts ; it is
quite conceivable that they may have very
little of bitterness or ill-will in them. What
is needed on behalf of peace is not that the
most conscientious and humane nations
should disable themselves from fighting ; but
that each nation should feel it to be wrong
and unworthy to seize on the possessions or
hurt the self-respect of other nations, and
that the neutral should be ready to incur
some risk and to bear some loss in coercing
the insolent and aggressive.

It is a part of our discipline that we should
have to struggle with contradictions and
confusions in working out the spiritual designs
of our Maker. The road towards perfection
is no smooth one. The great encouragement,
without which we could hardly persevere, is
to see that progress is possible, and is actually
being made. In trading and fighting with
each other men will indulge, we must expect,
the evil passions of covetousness and pride
and cruelty, they will call deceit and lies to
their aid ; but the spirit which God breathes
into his children has the task of purging trade
and exalting it into mutual help, of making

war more noble and humane and rare until it dies out. And the goal which the Christian sees before him as the necessary object of the Divine Purpose is a world made harmonious and happy by the all-conquering mind of brotherhood.

CHAPTER III

THE CIVIL ORDER OF HUMAN SOCIETY

In the last chapter we regarded the Catholic Church as representing the true and real relation of the human race to its invisible Head,—a relation which makes all men fellow-members together, and is the living root of the universal bonds and duties of humanity. We go on to consider how men, as social beings, find themselves further organised.

As we look around us, we see ourselves and our fellow-men gathered into groups of various kinds and sizes, called civil as distinct from those which are ecclesiastical or religious. The most characteristic feature of the civil order at the present stage of history is the tendency to largeness of grouping. It is an age of empires, of dominions vaster than have ever been known before, in the sphere of government; as, in the sphere of economics, it is the age of larger associations

for business. Within the last few years our
own country has included an empire in its
ancient realm, and the sovereign bears the
title of Queen and Empress; and we con-
template with amazement the imperial
responsibilities accumulated on the Crown
and the Parliament of Great Britain and
Ireland. Everywhere we see some movement of acquisition, absorption, federation;
and these things take place not by design,
hardly even through the workings of irrepres-
sible ambition, but under the pressure of the
course of things. Was there ever anything
more grandiose in the history of the world
than the recent partition of Africa by some
five European powers, summarily transacted
with the pen of diplomacy by mutual agreement between these powers? Will it be
possible for the great dominions of this age
to hold themselves together without breaking?
What new effects will they have upon the
peace, the commerce, the general development of mankind? These questions will be
answered in time by history. The God of
the world is preparing his own future; it is
he who makes us, and not we ourselves.
We shall move safely, in so far as we suffer

ourselves to be led by his guiding hand.
The more we see the strings of destiny
plainly taken out of our hands by the great-
ness and spontaneousness of the main movements of the world, the more are we thrown
back upon simple allegiance to the sceptre of
righteousness and love.

Let us turn from the largest of civil groups
to the smallest. The Family was never more
important, never more interesting to observers
and thinkers as the elementary unit of society,
than it is now. It was a natural mistake, but
it is held to be a demonstrated mistake, to
assume the family to be the actual primitive
germ of human society. The family appears
to have been originally confused in more pro-
miscuous aggregations of human beings. It
is rather to the honour of the family that its
distinctness and importance have grown with
the growth of civilisation. The one husband
and the one wife, and their children belonging
to them ; the husband and the wife keeping
to each other, the parents caring for their
children and the children honouring their
parents : this complex unit is a fixed and
to all appearance a permanent factor of the

most highly developed and happiest human
society.   To the Christian these relations
are sacred; and what a difference it makes
to the family if they are held to be sacred by
the members of it!   Mr. Herbert Spencer
may shew us that these relations prove
themselves most favourable on the whole
to the sustentation of the race; and this may
be to some the complete explanation of them.
The demonstration is one to be welcomed by
the Christian; it entirely falls in with his
view: but he sees more in the family than
the evolutionist does; and what he sees is
evidently favourable—to him it will seem indispensable—to the purest and most beautiful
and most delightful affections.   We learn from
our sacred books that the family is God's
creation; that the union of the marriage-pair
is a symbol and living expression of the union
between Christ and humanity; that a father
is a visible witness to the Divine Fatherhood,
and that children are trained by the habit of
looking up to the earthly parent to know in
some real manner the Father in heaven.
We think we are right in setting a value
upon tender and thoughtful and reverent
affections, and in reckoning these a precious

part of the total product of human existence ; and it seems to us that they are like a delicate vapour which would be chilled and precipitated by contact with the philosophy that sees in them nothing but the necessary outcome of the individual's desire of what is pleasant.

How to make the best of the family is one of the problems upon which opinion and legislation are in all advancing countries constrained to exercise themselves. Christian opinion is reasonably and rightly jealous of any innovation in custom or law which threatens to lower the relations of the home and to impair their vitality. But Christian opinion is not always wise ; it is seldom as free to learn as a stronger faith would enable it to be. And it is often very difficult for any one to know for certain what the effect of an innovation upon the family or home would be. The most emphatic and obtrusive Christian opinion is generally content to stand by tradition, and has thus been sometimes in opposition to changes which experience has ultimately proved to be beneficial. Many questions which are more or less pendent in these days of ours have their chief interest in their bearing upon the home. Compulsory

education, education by the State, public and
charitable relief of poverty, the concession to
women of instruction and public duties, the
enfranchisement of wives, liberty to marry a
deceased wife's sister, legal divorce, are of
this class. If any measure or custom promoted under one or other of these heads could
be demonstrated to be on the whole and in
the long run injurious to the family, Christian
feeling ought to be against it, and wise states-
manship would shrink from advocating it.
But it is a fact to be borne in mind, that the
removal of obstructions which have been
excusably defended as necessary safeguards
has often been the means of promoting a
higher, because a freer, moral life. The aim
to be kept in view is not a carefully fettered
home, but a growth of the higher kind of
spiritual or personal relations. Whatever
convictions and customs and laws will most
effectually build up the perfect family,—these
will not only be best for each family, but will
on that account be of the highest value to
human society in general.

If it may plainly be seen that advancing
civilisation bears its witness to that sacred-

ness of the Family which is one of the traditions of Christian belief, it is evident also that
the idea of the Nation, as a larger group of
human beings, holds its ground in these
days, and commands even more deference
from men's minds than it has ever received
before.   It is true that this appears to be an
age of empires; and some wise men have
dreaded the ideas of an empire as tending to
encroach upon and swallow up the characteristic consciousness of the nation.   According
to the Christian view, the Divine Maker is
seen to have planted men in families, in
tribal commonwealths or nations, and in the
universal community; these are the three
organisms which hold the first rank amongst
all the groupings of men, and by the authority
of which human duties are chiefly defined.
An empire of the old Oriental type, professedly founded on force, governed by
despotic rule, existing for the aggrandise-
ment of a single man or a dominant race,
careless of the forms of national life and of
the institutions which have availed to express
the mind of the people and to protect their
rights, has been odious to those who have
learnt to reverence the nation, and has been

regarded by them as a temporary agency of destruction and change. But the ways of Providence are not to be prescribed. And the aspect of the world at the present time seems to indicate that imperial magnitudes are not incompatible with national sentiment. There are empires and empires. It may be possible for an empire to be in effect a great nation. Or there may be a kind of distribution of the feelings and activities of national life, of the sense of a national calling and the duties proper to it, between smaller bodies or organisms within an empire and the empire as itself an organism. In-any case it belongs to Christian faith to learn the lessons of the present, rather than to cling to any tradition that is passing away.

If we try to define a nation, we discover that this is not a simple matter. And when nothing turns upon or is deduced from the definition, we need not embarrass ourselves with the obligation to define. But the irregularities of national development are so great, that it is difficult to use any particular nation for didactic purposes without stumbling into confusion. We should not like to be forbidden to speak of the English nation.

But we might at once be asked what populations the term includes. Do the Scottish
people form part of the English nation? Or
do they themselves constitute a Scottish
nation? The Nationalists of Ireland have
for their aim that the Irish people may
become a real and acknowledged nation:
ought we then to look for the essential points
of nationality in the legislation which is to
create a parliament and a ministry for that
country? By questions like these every
enthusiast for nationality might be put into
difficulties. There is no difficulty, however,
in imagining an ideal nation. We can think
of a population occupying a land enclosed
within defined boundaries, speaking the same
language, subject to one supreme governing
authority, using the same laws, looking back
over a common history, inheriting the same
glories, worshipping the same God: to a
people living under these conditions we
should unhesitatingly give the name of a
nation. And Christians will feel that there
is something high and entitled to respect in
this name. It is true that the idea of a
nation is less distinctively Christian, less
properly belongs to the New Covenant, than

that of the family, or that of the whole community of men. The age and world of the New Testament knew next to nothing of nations; and it was the peculiar task of the Apostles of Christ to proclaim the universal Divine kingdom, and to found the universal Divine society. But Christendom, in inheriting the Scriptures of the Old Covenant as sacred, has had for its continual study the history of a race made into a nation by their God. In the commonwealth of Israel the civil order is traced directly to Divine authority. And no people can read the Hebrew Scriptures with the old Jewish and Christian faith and not receive from them a strong influence upon its political mind. It is enough to quote the well-known words in which Milton, by the mouth of our Lord, places the prophets of Israel far above other statists and lovers of their country :—

> " As men divinely taught and better teaching
> The solid rules of civil government,
> In their majestic unaffected style,
> Than all the oratory of Greece and Rome.
> In them is plainest taught, and easiest learnt,
> What makes a nation happy, and keeps it so,
> What ruins kingdoms, and lays cities flat :
> These only, with our law, best form a king."

It is impossible that any ruler or politician
formed by the study of the law and the
prophets of Israel should not think of a
nation as having a Divine calling, and being
organically part of the Divine creation.
And though the Apostles, in an age when
national life was overwhelmed and thrown
into confusion, had little occasion for speaking of nations, we have in the New Testament continual recognition of civil government
as a ministry held under God. The law and
order even of the Roman Empire were from
God ; and every one who administered justice
was carrying out a portion of the will of
God. So that to Christians the civil order,
including the institutes of government and
defence and the administration of justice,
is a work of God ; and the more there
is of coherence and continuance and happiness in a commonwealth, the more plainly
will it seem to them to bear the impress
of the Divine hand. And the passion
which the idea of nationality is able in
these days to inspire, and the sacrifices
to which it impels, may be explained as
paying, however blindly and confusedly, the
homage due to the authority of that idea and

confessing it to be a part of the creative will
of God.   Patriotism, loyalty, is not a foolish
intoxication ; it may be the soberest self-
offering to the God of our country and of our
fathers.

CHAPTER IV

JUSTICE

THE name of justice is closely and necessarily associated with the idea of the nation or commonwealth ; and I go on to consider how the recognition of this organism of human society, as belonging by its essence to the invisible world, and having its origin and authority in God, bears upon the nature of justice and the questions connected with it.

Here again I may appeal to a passion by which the feelings of men are moved in an unprecedented degree at the present time. There is a certain dissatisfaction stirring and heaving in the mind of the general population, in this country, in the more advanced parts of Europe, in our colonies, and in the United States of America. It seems to many that a less unequal distribution of the things which men desire might be attained, and it is always assumed and declared that the attainment would be a triumph of justice. Justice is invoked without hesitation as an authority to which all men may be expected to pay deference, and to which those on whom it may inflict losses should submit with the best grace they can. When men are deprived of what they believe to be just, a singular emotion, such as easily finds vent in tears, is excited in susceptible natures. Together with the desire of improvement in the conditions of possession, there is a great anxiety to arrive at a more exact fulfilment of justice in all the other matters with which justice is concerned. The mental ease of innumerable persons is being continually disturbed by doubt whether this or that arrangement or transaction is as just as it might be. Never, I think it may be said, was justice more Divine to men than it is now.

This worship of justice, as a power which speaks with authority to the consciences of all men, is the more remarkable when we notice the extreme difficulty which men find in determining what justice means, and in agreeing upon any principle or method by which what is just is to be ascertained. It is easy to see that some dealings, whether in the shape of a division of things desired, or in that of an assignment of reward or punishment, are what all would admit to be unjust. But why they are unjust would not be so easily explained. It is when we try to make existing arrangements or customs more just that the difficulty confronts us in the most perplexing form. Take the apportionment of taxation for an example. What is the just principle of apportionment? It will be very generally agreed that it is just for all citizens to contribute something towards the expenses of government. But how are their respective contributions to be assessed? Is it just that a father of a family should pay more or that he should pay less than an unmarried man receiving the same income? The family man gets more from the government,—that is an argument on the one side; he has less to spare,—that is an argument on the other side. It sounds fair that all should contribute proportionately, though we might ask whether it should be in proportion to the property of each, or his income, or his expenditure, and whether the other claims on his means should be taken into account; but we are all inclined to favour the poor, and to most minds it would seem just to lay heavier burdens than the proportion of their means would assign on the rich than on the poor. Some would perhaps go so far as to say that it is contrary to ideal justice that any should be better off than others, and therefore that the State ought to do all that it can be constrained or enabled to do to level existing inequalities. It would be a convenient conclusion that the levying of taxes and rates is a matter to which justice does not apply. This, however, would be very unwillingly admitted. And it would be found that in other provinces there is similar difficulty in framing rules of self-evident justice; so that men might find themselves driven at last to the extremity of giving up the use of the words just and justice altogether.

Never were men less likely to do this than now. They are more deeply persuaded than ever that the regulation of human affairs ought to be in accordance with justice. The work of philosophers consists for the most part in making formulas for the modes of thought and action to which men are being really impelled by the progress of social development; and there is no question which human life is now putting more urgently to speculators than that which asks what is the nature of justice.

In all ages it seems to have been believed, by wise men and the multitude alike, that justice could be explained by equality. It has been declared by respectable authorities, and proclaimed in the face of the world, that men are equal, and that they have equal rights. Justice is held by many to be the giving to equal men of their equal rights. There must be something in this notion of equality to account for the sway which it has obtained over the minds of men. But the moment you lean upon it for support it proves itself no better than a broken reed. There is a certain rough classing of people together which is found necessary for the purposes of external administration; some protection against arbitrary and oppressive behaviour has been found in the rule that persons were to be treated alike; and it looks as if this were the ground, and the only ground, for the homage paid to equality. But men are obviously not equal; they are not born equal, any more than they become so. There is nothing to support an assumption that the Creator meant or means them to be equal. The whole structure of human society appears rather, one may say, to be built upon inequality. Where the law treats persons in the same way, it is easy to see that its justice is imperfect, precisely because it cannot take account of the real inequality of the persons. Perfect justice will be characteristically unequal, because it will observe with careful discrimination the endless differences that actually exist in persons and in circumstances. It seems disrespectful to a widespread belief to dismiss equality as an impostor; but I have failed to see any light thrown by it upon the essential nature of justice.

A partial explanation of the common feeling about justice may no doubt be found in the authority which *Law* exercises over the general mind. The justice with which men are concerned in actual life is to a very large extent that of the law. Possession which the law recognises is assumed as a matter of course, by the possessor at least, to be just possession; and any forcible interference with it is resented. The law punishes crime, and to get an offender legally punished is said to be to bring him to justice. It is an obvious account of justice, therefore, to define it as being what the law prescribes. Law will have to be itself accounted for; but that may be done without bringing in the idea of justice: and then the ultimate explanation of justice might be sought in referring it to the law. There are two defects in this explanation. (1) There is a considerable part of life with which the laws do not interfere; and men habitually think and speak of acts and arrangements in spheres outside the law as being just or unjust. Indeed in our ordinary speech we seem rather to limit the use of these words to extra-legal action. We do not speak of an assault or a burglary as unjust. We say that a schoolmaster is unjust when he favours one boy in a class; that an employer is unjust if he binds a man to the fulfilment of a legal engagement made in ignorance or misunderstanding. (2) It is also habitual to speak of laws themselves as being just or unjust. In these days men consciously and with much effort make laws;

they repeal old laws and add new ones : and it is the professed aim of legislators to render the law as just as possible ; that is, to bring it into conformity with a standard of justice assumed to be antecedent to it and above it.

But the philosophy of evolution is that with which we all have to reckon. Most well-informed persons are feeling now that they must at least find room in their scheme of things for the chief principles and conclusions of the theory—if it is not rather to be called the science—of evolution. And this philosophy has spoken definitely, by the mouth of its most illustrious exponent, on the subject of justice. Mr. Herbert Spencer is expressly engaged in setting forth the origin and nature and applications of justice in a work of which he has already published the earlier portion ;[1] and it is impossible not to recognise that his analysis and history have a great deal of truth in them. He traces justice, as he traces everything, to the one primal instinctive force, the desire of what is agreeable. This is originally a solitary force, dwelling in the single individual.

[1] See the *Nineteenth Century* for March and April 1890.

Every man, every animal, is an organism desiring what is pleasant and striving to get it. Out of this impelling desire all the virtues have grown. This primal desire has led, in a way which can be described and explained, to the creation of society, and the development of all social habits. I am giving Mr. Spencer's view; but as one which undeniably accords with facts which we must all acknowledge. In very early times it became evident that a living being might obtain more pleasure by co-operating with other living beings than by standing alone. Thus society began. One living being can directly give pleasure to another; but it is chiefly for the two objects of defence and of economy of production that men have associated themselves together. Smaller groups have become larger, that they may defend themselves the better, and that they may produce more of what men like and more easily. By the primal instinct, the strong man makes use of his strength for his own advantage; but several together, though they may be separately less strong, are stronger than the strongest. And, to make association possible, individuals must consent to some restrictions upon their pursuit of what they like. To live and work together, individuals must be at peace; and they will not be at peace if all are, without restriction, trying to get, at their neighbour's expense, the most of what pleases them. By degrees the interest of the society, though it has for its original and only rational foundation the desire of the individual, becomes predominant. Individuals are sacrificed freely by the will of the larger number to the interest of the society; and, what is more remarkable, they are actually so wrought upon that they sacrifice themselves. A curious topsey - turveyism of nature! Self-sacrifice comes of the force of habit. The interest of the society obtains in the course of long ages a dominant power over the collections of feelings called minds; and the self-seeking animal, through the sole development of self-pleasing habits, is led to do the opposite of pleasing self. That is the simple explanation of all human life as we see it now. And justice is the actual relation, the relation which the progress of the race produces, between the activities of single persons pursuing their own pleasure, and the restrictions imposed upon the activities of each by the simultaneous activities of others living with them. The balance or compromise is not always the same ; it varies at different stages of human progress ; but what is always meant by justice is the ratio or equilibrium or resultant produced at each moment by the struggle for what pleases, between the self-seeking of the individual and the restrictions imposed upon it by the simultaneous self-seeking of fellow-members of the society. The philosopher, observing the course of things, can watch how either of these forces, the impelling and the restraining, gets a little the better of the other ; he perceives how the sustentation of the race, which is the combination of the prosperities of individuals, is on the one hand favoured by the freedom of the individual, which gives advantages to strength and superiority, and how on the other hand it is favoured by the restraining influence of the community, which secures concord and preserves the weaker from being crushed.

These observations are full of instruction ; they throw light on the manner in which the accepted rules of justice have been evolved.

But this philosophy of Mr. Spencer's is purely
naturalistic, and has no title to be called ethical. The ideas of right, duty, obligation, are
foreign to it; the names represent conceptions
which this philosophy pronounces to be illusions. Mr. Spencer and other thinkers of
his school persist in using the common moral
phraseology; in truth they cannot help it;
no man can hold converse with other men
without using it. But they use it illegiti-
mately; they are denying their own principles whilst they use it. It is astonishing
that they can endure this perpetual self-
contradiction. Let me quote a recent
statement ˙of Mr. Spencer's, made in the
very face of this problem. "If you ask
what prompts me to denounce our unjust
treatment of inferior races, I reply that I
am prompted by a feeling which is aroused
in me quite apart from any sense of duty,
quite apart from any thought of Divine com-
mand, quite apart from any thought of reward
or punishment here or hereafter. In part
the feeling results from consciousness of the
suffering inflicted, which is a painful consciousness, and in part from irritation at the
breach of a law of conduct on behalf of which

my sentiments are enlisted, and obedience to which I regard as needful for the welfare of humanity in general. If you say that my theory gives me no reason for feeling this pain, the answer is that I cannot help feeling it ; and if you say that my theory gives me no reason for my interest in asserting this principle, the answer is that I cannot help being interested."[1] "Quite apart from any sense of duty"; "I cannot help feeling the pain, the interest." Yes, that is a frank statement of the beginning and end of this philosophy. Feelings come by nature, the feelings which we call moral among the rest. One man cannot help feeling generous ; another cannot help feeling greedy and cruel. The sense of duty is an illusion. Certainly, anything less calculated to carry authority to the conscience, and bring a sense of duty to bear upon it, than the varying balance between the self-seeking of the individual and the self-seeking of the aggregate of other individuals could not easily be imagined. Even if this balance could show us satisfactorily how all

---

[1] This is quoted from a letter which Mr. Spencer kindly wrote to me, and which was published, with his permission, in the (London) *Guardian*, 6th August 1890.

the common notions of what is just between
man and man are formed, one chief thing
which we want to know is why justice speaks
with authority to the universal conscience.

Some of those who uphold a real but non-
theological morality would speak of the idea
of justice as involved in the constitution of
the human mind. They pay homage to this
idea as independent, as immutable, as belonging in some essential way to the higher nature
of man. There is something in ourselves,
they hold, which will tell us what is just if
we will listen to it ; and our moral nature
makes it our duty to listen to it. Others
would say that justice consists in the arrangements which are best for society, and that in
virtue of our moral nature the good of society
is a law and ideal for the individual. These
doctrines of a transcendental morality are
high and draw us upwards, but they leave on
many minds an uncomfortable impression of
vagueness and arbitrariness. The phrases
independent and immutable, though they
commend themselves to our reverence and
our sense of obligation, hardly agree with
what experience proves to be the progressive

nature of morality.   Nor is it satisfactory to
all of us to be thrown back on our own minds
as an ultimate authority.   We would rather
depend upon something that does not so evade
and fail us as our own natures are apt to do,
something to which we could more confidently
appeal in praising and condemning, in exhort-
ing and coercing, our fellow-men.

If we take courage to assume—we to
whom the assumption is a possible one—
that there is an Unseen Power, a Living
God, whose creatures and children we are,
who is training by his own methods and for
his own ends the race which he has brought
into existence, and whose will we have some
trustworthy means of knowing, these conclusions amongst others will follow: we shall
understand the unity and community of men ;
the meaning of progress, and its harmony
with order, will become apparent to us ; and
we shall perceive ourselves to be subject to a
government the authority of which it would
be absurd to call in question.   And we are
led on to the apprehension of justice as being
essentially the order in which the Maker con-
stitutes the civil groups of men ; in one sense

the aggregate of the relations, in another sense the fulfilling of the relations, in which the Maker of all binds men to one another and to the things around them.

This is the idea of justice which we find running through the Bible. The Anglo-Saxon word "righteous" is used more commonly in both Testaments than the Latin word "just"; and it is due perhaps to this biblical use that righteousness has come to mean to our ears something both wider and more religious than justice : but in the Bible itself no distinction between them is intended. One of the questions raised by any inquiry concerning justice, and one which puts itself especially to believers in the Bible, is in what sense we can speak of the Supreme God as Himself righteous or just. It was the chief thought of the children of Israel concerning their God Jehovah, that He was just or righteous : what did they mean in so describing Him ? The first answer would probably be that they regarded Him as rendering to every man according to his works. But this was rather what they were sure a righteous God would do than that which constituted His righteousness. They did not profess to

understand fully what God's rewards were,
or the methods of his distribution of them.
What they felt in praising Jehovah as the
righteous God was that he was a Ruler who
might be trusted, a Ruler whose dealings
with them, if they knew all, would commend
themselves to their consciences and under-
standings as being for the best.   They
believed, with much experience to sustain
the belief, but with some also that perplexed
it, that if they served him by keeping loyally
the regulations made for their commonwealth,
they would prosper, and that if they behaved
disloyally and licentiously, they would suffer.
Jehovah was a Ruler who might be trusted
without reserve.   That is, he was essentially
a God of order.   The order of the physical
universe was from him; the moral or spiritual
order of human society was from him.   All
relations between man and man which proved
themselves happy and wholesome were his
ordinances, and he sustained those relations
and promoted the fulfilment of them by
rewards and punishments.

In the New Testament, St. Paul is the
exponent of a profound and fruitful idea
concerning Divine and human righteousness.

He held with peculiar intensity the old Jewish belief in righteousness, and the righteousness in which he believed was essentially practical. No man was to be called righteous unless he acted righteously : God's righteousness was such as would certainly manifest itself in rendering to every man according to his works. But it was revealed to St. Paul that the inner nature of man was such, and he was so related to the God who made him, that he could only be right by looking up to God and submitting to him and allowing himself to be made the trustful agent of the Divine will. One who set himself to walk in his own way, and who made himself his only master, was sure to go wrong and to fail. The strength and success of man's life were to be found in filial dependence and sur-render and conformity. Human righteous-ness or justice came through submission to the righteousness or justice of God. This was St. Paul's theory of justification. And in his philosophy of justice we may again see the idea of order glorified. The world to his eye is built up out of orderly relations pro-ceeding from and sustained by the one living Creative Power ; and the law for each man is that he should keep the place and do the work assigned to him. He will find the place and the work, and receive the sufficiency he needs, through humility, teachableness, reverence,—in a word, through faith. This, then, is what we learn from the Bible, —that God is just in being the author and maintainer of the spiritual order of the universe, and that human justice is the due observance and fulfilment of the relations which God creates.

Substantially the same explanation of justice is given in the most famous of all books on this subject, Plato's treatise called *The Commonwealth, or, Concerning Justice.* By a method of inquiry which may strike a reader as artificial, but which proves itself rich in interesting suggestions, Plato comes to the conclusion that Justice is the principle by which each class and every member of the commonwealth are kept in their places—in the places, that is, which the prosperity and happiness of the commonwealth as a whole would assign to them. Plato set the society, the commonwealth, above the individual, and he thought he saw in the constitution of the

community an enlarged form of the nature
of the single man. He compared the ruling
class with the reason, the fighting class with
the combative emotions, the industrial class
with the appetites; and as social justice
appeared to him to be the principle which
kept the classes of the commonwealth in
their respective relations and places, and so
maintained the harmony and well-being of
the community, he was led to explain justice
in the individual, by analogy, as the principle
which kept the reason, the emotions, and the
appetites in their proper relations, and so
produced the well-balanced man, the man at
peace in himself. We shall prefer to this
account St. Paul's idea, that justice in the
man is conformity to the spiritual order by
which he is environed. But we may claim
Plato as maintaining and illustrating the
truth that the explanation of Justice is to
be found in the moral order of which the
living Creator of mankind is the Author. It
is in this explanation that we discover the
ultimate reason of the authority with which
justice speaks to the human mind, an
authority which seems to increase with the
development of human society, and which is

forcing itself on our attention so strongly at the present time.

In the age of Plato there was evidently the same sort of difficulty as there is now in understanding justice. He mentions some of the lower views of it to which men were led by inquiry and analysis at that time. Justice was said to be the interest of the stronger,[1] of those who obtained the mastery in a society. These made the laws for their own advantage, and the carrying out of the laws was called justice. Another view[2] was that justice consisted in the compromise between the appetitive activities of the individual and the appetitive activities of his neighbours, or the regulated equilibrium of individual freedom and social restriction,— which is precisely the explanation of justice which Mr. Herbert Spencer is now engaged in elaborating. If either of these explanations is adopted as adequate, the veil of regal authority is torn from justice, and it is exposed as a false pretender. No one can reverence the naked interest of the stronger, or appeal to it with passion as a law which

[1] *The Republic*, book i. p. 338.
[2] *Ibid.* book ii. pp. 358, 359.

ought to commend itself to the consciences of his neighbours. Nor do we feel moved to bow with moral conviction before the mere resultant of conflicting appetites. But if the moral authority of justice is derived from the will of the Creator who is working out the perfection and happiness of human society, that authority may be seen to back up even the interest of the stronger and the equilibrium of struggling desires. There can be no practical justice without coercive law, and coercive law cannot be enforced except by those who have strength to rule. As soon as administration becomes efficient and prosperous, justice is sure to prevail in some tolerable degree, whether the rule be that of an African chief or that of a civilised democracy. And rule becomes stronger as its administration is more orderly. Similarly the willing subjection of desires in the individual to the restrictions imposed upon them by the combined desires of others is a homage rendered to order, that is, to justice, or to the regulating will of the Creating Power who cares for the good of all. If we desire to interrogate the instinctive feelings of mankind as to the nature of justice, we may trace the idea of order in the two great synonyms right and just. For right, *rectum*, probably means ruled in the sense of straight rather than in that of enacted by force. And just, from *jus*, appears to mean what is joined or fitted, or—as we say—adjusted. Equal also, *aequum*, I am inclined to suggest, may have derived its original authority from its primary sense of evenness. Straight, fit, even—these terms all describe orderly arrangement; and they express the natural feeling of the early societies of men about what is just.

Behind any systematic equilibrium of the moment which is felt to give satisfaction and comfort to human minds and to be helping forward harmonious co-operation and the building up of society, men have always had some conception, however vague it may have been and however little they may have known how to describe it, of something better in ad-justment and harmony than the best which has yet been realised. The dissatisfaction which is indispensable to improvement and progress has been nourished by this vision. Men and societies of men have always lived upon Promise; and when the breath of Hope, responsive to Divine Promise, fails to breathe perpetually upon their minds, they fall into torpor and decay. The advanced communities of the present age are blessed with wonderful benefits of justice, but the restlessness of humane and sympathetic natures, pouring out complaints and reproaches against what they perceive to be unequal and unsatisfactory in our relations to one another and the things around us, is a token and witness that the God of mankind has not finished his work but is preparing yet nobler and more perfect developments of it.

CHAPTER V

THOSE who deny themselves the advantage of referring to the Divine will as the ground and explanation of morality, and who are at the same time unwilling that morality should be regarded as nothing more than the result of experience, are led to ascribe authority to the moral law by declaring it to be absolute and immutable, entitled by what it is eternally in itself to the respect and obedience of mankind. Except for the prestige thus obtained for morality, it would seem better, as being more in accordance with observed facts, to think of morality as progressive. If justice, for example, is to be regarded as an absolute and immutable law, having a natural authority to the human mind, it must be something so vague and intangible that it will hardly be serviceable for guidance ; and practical persons will be tempted to pronounce it to be a metaphysical *eidolon*, a projection of what men happen to be for the time accepting as just arrangements. We learn from the history of mankind that men's conceptions of what is just have varied greatly in time and place,—have in fact grown with the growth of civilisation. And the view of justice according to which it means, as a law, the aggregate of the relations of civil society, and, as a habit, the fulfilment of those relations, has this advantage, that it expects justice to make advances as human society is developed.

Some assumptions which have been confidently insisted upon, but which have been productive of confusion, are disposed of by this view. We cannot hold that there are any absolute rights of man. Instead of entering into controversy as to the specification of such rights, and maintaining that certain rights may be properly, whilst others are improperly, claimed for man, we shall know of no rights inhering either in man as man, or in any man as an individual. Men's rights will be such securities and liberties as are assigned to them, to speak most simply,

by the law ; or, to allow for some laws
being behind the age, by the best general
judgments of the community at the stage of
development to which it has been brought.
There are many, perhaps, who would unwillingly give up the notion that freedom, for
example, is a natural right of man ; though
the unwillingness will be less if they have
tried to define natural freedom, and have lost
themselves in the hopeless difficulties of the
attempt.　But we, knowing nothing of
freedom as a natural right, shall not be
hampered by any necessity of pronouncing
what the freedom is which nature bestows on
man ; to us freedom will be a kind of elbow-
room required for the performance of the
parts assigned to a man by the constitution
of the society in which he finds himself.
Even slavery, such as makes a human being
an article of sale and purchase, we cannot
denounce as the violation of a natural right.
The essential injustice of slavery will be that
it is incompatible with the duties of a member
of a family and of a commonwealth.　If we
should hear it affirmed that the private owning of land is contrary to eternal justice, the
allegation will be to us not so much untrue

as without meaning ; whilst at the same time the claim of any person to hold something which he has inherited or acquired, as made his by absolute justice, will be a vain imagination. Questions of possession are not to be settled by reference to an absolute and eternal justice, because the justice which we know is dependent and progressive.

How then are we to find out what is just?

We must have the courage to conclude that, on many points as to which men have eagerly claimed the authority of an imperative justice for arrangements which they have desired or approved, there is no intelligible decree of justice to be heard. As to possessions, contracts, assessments, remuneration, punishments, we cannot profess to know any rules or standard, to have access to any oracle, of abstract justice. If it be said that justice requires that men should have this and that, should pay or be paid so much, should have so much punishment inflicted on them, we have to admit that, apart from law and custom and the good of the community, we have no rule for determining just ownership, just wages, just prices, just penalties. We cannot allow ourselves the satisfaction of affirming that justice requires that one man should be as well off as another, or that every man should have the environment that will be most favourable for his development, or that a poor man should have a vote as well as a rich man, or a woman as well as a man, or that no man should receive lower wages than will keep him and his family at a certain level of comfort. It is one thing to cherish aspirations after universal happiness, another thing to assume that, so long as the universal happiness is not realised, there are personal wrongs which the community is bound and able to redress. When we consider how freely and confidently claims are made in the name of absolute justice for what we should gladly welcome as improvements, we may well feel reluctant to forego the support which the name of justice gives to a demand. It seems almost pathetic, for example, that those who may be insisting, as if the thing were as clear as day, that justice requires that certain labour should be paid for at the rate of 6d. an hour, should have to be asked why justice does not rather fix the payment at 9d. or 1s. an hour.

There are certain principles, however,

which, from the point of view of a progressive Divine order of the world, we may bring to bear upon human affairs, in the hope of securing such justice as is possible and real.

(1) If we regard the authority of justice as being that of the order in which the Creator is constituting and developing human society, it will be inevitable that we should pay an almost unqualified deference to the regulations sanctioned at any time by law and custom. And this respect for law will be in accordance with the common and universal feeling about justice. The first notion of men everywhere as to what is just is, that it is what the law prescribes or sanctions,—that the just man is he "qui consulta patrum, qui leges juraque servat." The authority of law and the belief in justice have grown simultaneously in historic communities. So that it has been easy for disputers to maintain that the whole explanation of justice is to be found in this account of it,—that it is the arrangement made by law, and that to be just is to obey the law. The anti-moral arguer in the *Republic* of Plato, accepting that definition and pushing inquiry a step further, was able to contend that justice meant the interest

of the stronger ; for the law, he argued, was made by those who had power in a community, and they naturally made such rules as were for their own advantage. There is a great deal of truth in these statements, cynical as they may appear. The laws in force at any time in any land will always indicate by the bias of their favour what class is there and at that time holding the chief power ; or, if we take the persistency of laws into account, we should rather say, what class had for some time previous to the given moment been holding the chief power. But the rules which seem to us as we look back upon them to have been prompted by the selfish interest of the stronger are so much better than the absence of laws, and the enforcement of such rules is so much better than the absence of an enforcing power, that even under what we should call an oppressive régime we should find it reasonable to associate, if we could not quite identify, justice with legality. What men chiefly want, in living their lives, is to know what they can depend upon. This is what makes the uniformity of the laws of nature so indispensable a basis of human life and progress. Philo-

sophers have discovered that the laws of
nature are cruel, and there are some speculators who expatiate with enjoyment upon
the unmoral tyranny of the God of nature ;
but these laws work uniformly, and men learn
that they can depend upon them, and this
trustworthiness more than compensates for
the alleged cruelty. And so the first thing
necessary for progressive life in a community
is that there should be an administration upon
which men can calculate, that they should
know to what arrangements they have to
adjust their plans and efforts, with what ex-
pectations they may look forward to the
future. It is uncertainty, arbitrariness, that
afflicts men with a sense of injustice, and
paralyses the provident endeavours on which
progress and prosperity depend. I do not
admit, however, that human laws are at any
time more than in part the expression of the
selfish desires of the stronger ; they are the
result of many impulses and movements in
human life : what I urge is that laws, or
customs having the force of laws, are the
actual form in which the Creator is making
human society ; and that therefore justice is,
both in fact and reasonably, to a very large

extent, the same thing as legality. It is in accordance with our faith in an orderly Divine development that justice should be to us what our fathers were led to enforce.

(2) But there is another principle which the same faith equally commends to our attention. We can recognise a justice superior to laws because the order which finds expression in laws is a spiritual and growing order. The will of the Maker is that we should know and fulfil the relations in which he constructs his human world ; and he is continually developing those relations into a greater complexity and a more satisfying harmony. There is much fulfilment of these relations which transcends the sphere of coercive law ; and the coercive law of a community must of itself be continually improved by a progressive race. St. Paul, full of the faith in an ordering Lord, lays down the duty of the child in these words : " Children, obey your parents in the Lord, for this is just " ; whilst in the twin-passage he writes, " Children, obey your parents in all things, for this is well-pleasing in the Lord." Obedience to parents belongs for the most part to supra-legal duty, and can only in the lower and

superficial degree be the subject of coercive laws; but also the laws relating to it have needed and have received continual improvement. What the Romans thought just with regard to the subjection of children to fathers seems to us now no better than barbarous. There are races of men whose laws are very stationary; but those races are themselves in the rest of their life similarly stationary. Races that advance will find it necessary to modify their laws. I have said that the feeling for justice keeps pace with the authority of law amongst any people; and I infer, therefore, that the enthusiasm in demanding justice which is characteristic of our time is a sign that our laws commend themselves in no ordinary degree to the general mind, and have a powerful influence over it. But it is also true that we perceive amongst us indications of a somewhat restless eagerness to change the existing order. This desire of improvement we must admit to be from God. It bears witness to a creative power, working in men's lives and in history, which purposes to make human society better than it is. The existing order is good for its time; that there should be order at all is the thing

supremely good : but we may hope for a
better order than that in which we now have
our part. We cannot see distinctly far ahead;
but we are taught to look for more of harmony and health throughout the whole body,
for a condition in which the members, fulfilling
their respective offices with more enjoyment,
will also make more valuable contributions to
the common well-being. Any modifications
of the social system which will be favourable
to a really better social condition should find
us ready, as soon as our eyes are opened to
the recognition of them, to accept and promote them. And it will be just, or justice will
demand, that the changes of law and custom
that may be thus indicated should be made.

(3) But there is a third principle which
will claim our attention,—that social changes,
when seen to be desirable, should be made
with as little of disturbance and friction as
possible. The infinite value which we find
in order and in the reign of law involves this
principle.

It is impossible for us to admit that a
right of undisturbed possession inheres in any
man, or that individual ownership is the basis
of society. Statements to that effect are

freely made, but the belief they express is a mischievous error, and the needs or interests of society have constantly repudiated it. The only title to possession which a man has is that which is given to him by the order of society speaking through the law of the land; and that which law has given, law has reasonably asserted the right to take away. After all, it is no harder upon a man that the interest of the community, sought deliberately through a well-considered piece of legislation, should modify his possession of anything, than that his property should be affected, as it is every day, by non-legal changes which are due to some desire of the public, and which effectually alter values without altering laws. There are those who hold, with an unthinking sort of positiveness, that a man has an absolute right to anything which he happens to have received or obtained; a certain number of persons—Mr. Henry George and his disciples—hold that a man has a right to possess anything except land. With the latter class we can agree about the exception: we can see that no man has an absolute right to the ownership of a piece of land; but we must maintain that no man has an absolute right to the ownership of any other things. What we have further to urge, with regard to the owning of land and other things alike is, that the orderliness of life, which is justice, requires that present legal possession should be treated with the utmost respect that is compatible with the Creator's purpose of progress. Where possession is grossly abused, it may be necessary or desirable, in the interests of that justice which is the improved order of things immediately ahead of us, that its rights should be roughly interfered with; there have been states of national life in which revolutionary violence has been inevitable. But to our own country the inestimable blessing has been given of changes made with the least possible disturbance. The changes made at various times in our laws and customs have been very great; they could easily be so exhibited as to seem revolutionary; in our own time they have been both considerable and rapid. They are chiefly such as have been naturally involved in the transference of power from the few to the many; but there have been changes also which we should not as a matter of course call democratic, such as those relating to trade and religion and the

position of women.   As a rule, these changes
have been made after full discussion and
consideration, on the ground that they were
for the advantage of the whole community,
and with a very tender regard for existing
rights and prepossessions.   And we have had
our reward in a feature of English history
which strikes every observer, that the whole
population has acquiesced in the changes
after they have been made, and that reaction-
ary movements are virtually unknown in this
country.   If we may innocently indulge in
the boast, we may say that ideal justice
requires that social modifications should be
carried out in the future in the same manner
in which it has been the custom and the
happiness of the English nation to carry
them out in the past.

It is chiefly through the displeasure caused
by unjust acts that we are led to think about
justice; as it is illness that makes us think
about health.   We call certain acts unjust—
acts by which any one is deprived of advantages which properly belong to him—not,
ultimately, because they sin against rights
or claims inherent in individuals, but because
they are disorderly, violations of the order of

society. The feeling of resentment in an individual against injustice done to him arises in part from that instinctive primary desire to have and to get which to the evolutionist philosophy is the single force of life; but it is also in part the indignant resistance of the social body to disintegrating and destructive action, and to a violation of the will of its Maker. And it is one result of experience, one important feature of advancing civilisation, that it is felt to be of the highest importance that the forcible prevention and punishment of injustice should be taken out of the hands of the individual who thinks himself to be wronged, and placed in the charge of the community. All men have been brought to believe that they judge most truly about wrong when they regard it as done still more against the social body and its Maker than against the single person.

The contemplation, therefore, of justice or of injustice, as we have understood them, will keep our thoughts fixed upon the well-being—the harmony and health and growth —of the social body. The real guide to justice is the well-being of the community.

If we adapt our conceptions and language to this principle we shall seem perhaps to be losing something of directness and definiteness of appeal in ceasing to insist upon the natural rights of man and of men, but the loss will be only apparent; we shall in reality be rescued from some seriously misleading confusions. We cannot assume that inequality, as such, is unjust; we perceive that equality is impossible, that—like the threatened equilibrium of the solar system—it would be death. It would be a great gain if this were thoroughly realised in our social agitations. And it will conduce similarly to clearness of view and soundness of action if rights are understood to originate in the social body and not in the separate members of it. It might sound monstrous to many persons if they were told abruptly that they have no rights; but it would be really much simpler and better if all could attain to the true Christian consciousness of having no rights, except such as are needed and assigned for the fulfilment of their respective duties in their respective places. It would be chimerical to attempt to abolish or repudiate the phraseology of personal rights ; but it is not impossible to acquire the habit of thinking of rights as assigned and defined by the laws, that is ultimately by the well-being, of the social body.

And those who dwell upon the satisfactory justice of the future as consisting in the ful- filled relations of the ever-improving social order will be drawn into an habitual temper of unselfish hope. The Christian must be- lieve in his God, the Father of Jesus Christ, as a Power leading things onward. He per- ceives a Divine energy working without haste but without rest in the movements of the world. The Christian's God is entitled the God of hope ; and it is one of our most characteristic privileges to abound in hope. And our hope is of the glory of God ; that is, of the diffusion of a heavenly light, such as that which shines in the face of Jesus Christ, to be manifested expressly in the sphere of human life. Christians may well therefore be the fanatics of progress, per- sistently believing in it, ready to give them- selves for it. For they can understand how it may be the privilege of an individual to sacrifice worldly advantages to which he might have clung, or which he might have pursued, in order to serve the Creator's high purpose and to help more effectually in the building up of the body. And they will be ready to learn from the past, and to watch all indications pointing to the future, so that they may throw their endeavours trustfully into whatever may seem to be the appointed line of human development, and may go forward without timid apprehensions.

When we think of social improvement, it is inevitable that we should have chiefly in view the raising of the lower members of the social body. Though it is not they only who need to be improved, it is their condition that troubles and pains us most. But that of the many who are a little above this class we cannot but feel to be also such as should make us uneasy. For many years all anxious Christians have been thinking and trying how the lowest may be made happier fellow-members of the body. The name of Philanthropy has been given to the endeavour to raise by various schemes these classes which excite our compassion. It is beginning to be said on behalf of these classes that they want, not charity or philanthropy, but justice.

The meaning of those who use the phrase may generally be that wages ought to be raised at the expense of either the employer or the consumer. But there is a deeper sense in which the saying may be instructively interpreted. The action of philanthropy is not such as we should call orderly; it sees evils, and catches at abnormal expedients for promptly abolishing them. Its tendency is for the most part to weaken domestic and social ties in its endeavours to heal the miseries of the individual. It is confident, and sometimes arrogant and indocile, on the strength of its good intentions; but its schemes deserve to be described, in an expressive word, as demoralising. There is therefore a lamentable deduction to be made from the good which philanthropy does on the one hand to those who labour generously in its work, and on the other hand in some happy instances to the individual objects of it. The best influences are those which tend in any way to strengthen the ties of the home and of the social system, and to promote the due fulfilment of them. Better health of the body is what is wanted more than all sorts of salves and plasters and stimulant potions.

Whatever nourishes the self-respect and the sense of duty of the careless and the desponding, whatever sustains their faltering perseverance, is worth infinitely more than the gifts of indulgent sympathy. Not charity, in the sense of weakening indulgence or disintegrating experiments; but justice, in the sense of the due fulfilment of natural relations, is what is needed for the effective raising of the low. And to support this, a certain discipline of restraint and constraint, some use of what is rigorous and painful by the hands of God and men, may be more valuable than philanthropy.

Self-respect, respect for others, trust, hope, fear,—these are the steady levers of social elevation, these are the powers by which the Divine Spirit works towards social improvement in the hearts of men. Those who have been led to think thus of human development, whilst they turn away with feelings which I hardly like to characterise from the deification of nature and the doctrine that human and other animals are impelled by greed only, cannot adopt the assumption that the one thing needful, the one aim into which all the efforts of the humane ought to

be thrown, is to take away from the richer
and give to the poorer, and by arbitrary
economic processes to make the conditions
of different classes less unequal. They may
be perfectly willing that the rich should be
made less rich, so long as it is not done in
ways which will also have the effect of making
the poor poorer, a danger which only the
ignorant will despise ; they may earnestly
desire that the poor should become less poor,
and be thankful that this process has been
going on so steadily and so universally
during the last half century, and count with
joyful confidence upon the continuance of
this movement : but they will not put their
faith in a more equal economic distribution
as the effective power of social reform.
They may incur taunts from those whom
they recognise as honest friends of the less
fortunate classes, but who may scorn them
as hypocritical religionists if they profess to
care for those classes without being ready to
join in agitating for an economic revolution ;
but they cannot be false to what they see
and know. They must retain the old faith
that the world of mankind is a spiritual
creation. They are bound to bear witness

that the spiritual is above and beneath the physical ; that the Creator of mankind has a higher happiness in view for men than that of bodily comfort ; that you cannot raise men by only making it easier to them to get what their appetites crave, but that individuals will probably, and communities certainly, become more comfortable if they are enabled to be more dutiful.

And they will refuse to regard suffering as the worst of evils. They have learnt from history, their own personal experience confirming the lesson, that the permission of suffering is one of the methods by which the Creator produces what is best in human life. How, they will ask, can any one know anything of the world and not perceive that this is so? They cannot hear without impatience what is said in kindly excuse of the drunkard and the pauper, that it is impossible for men and women to be good in the low parts of our great cities. "Love have they found in huts where poor men lie." To them it is far more certain that faith and hope can triumph over pinching poverty in the lowest localities than that higher wages will wean men from the self-indulgence which issues in brutality and misery.

It is in truth a little wonderful that persons who know anything of themselves and of other men should be fascinated by schemes which are to make all indiscriminately comfortable, and which obviously tend to weaken the responsibility of grown men for themselves and for their families. No more responsibility! No more struggling! Well, for a moment, perhaps, that watchword may seem to promise welcome relief. As regards the conditions of the life to come, Christendom in general has provisionally accepted this cry. But, for the life with which we are familiar, moral responsibility is one of the surest evidences of the high origin of human nature ; it is through struggling that the best in man has been produced. Without conflict, without combative effort, what would the human race have been ? By being strained in hard exercise, the limbs and organs of the body acquire strength and pliability and adroitness. It has been in the struggling periods of national life, when men were wakeful and combative and aspiring, that the higher capacities of the intellect have been developed. And to struggle is never quite painless, though at times the sensation of pain may be lost in the pleasurable excitement of aroused effort. "There be some sports are painful, and their labour Delight in them sets off." Pain unlulled by such excitement, pain that is felt, has of itself a certain power to disencumber the mind of nonsense, and to give keenness to the vision and energy and pathos to expression ; so that we are accustomed to think of the highest art having its birth through travail-pangs,— of men cradled into poetry by wrong, who learn in suffering what they teach in song. And in the spiritual region, who are the men that interest us most and attract our deepest reverence ? Is it not they who have striven and suffered ? What sort of admiration have we for the type of man who would be the perfect product of a civilisation in which everything should be made smooth for every one, the man who has never had an anxiety, who has never had an effort called forth by necessity or resistance ? It has been the lot of the sons of men, as well as of the Son of man, to be made perfect through suffering.

I do not forget that it might be said, " Do

you wish, then, to preserve wrongs and
anxieties and miseries, as the rich preserve
game, that men may be exercised by them,
and so may bring forth the fruit of righteousness? Are we not all at one in trying to
make the conditions of human life smoother
and more agreeable for all?" I admit that
we are confronted here by a speculative
problem of some difficulty. If it is by toil of
heart and knees and hands that heights are
scaled and shining table-lands reached, how
will it be with those who live when every
valley shall be exalted and every mountain
and hill shall be made low, and the crooked
shall be made straight and the rough places
plain? If we advance towards nobler states
through honest and earnest conflict with evil,
what is to become of us when we have successfully put down evil? That is a question
to which no conclusive answer can be given.
It is a familiar difficulty to those who try to
realise the life of just men made perfect. It
is one of the problems which drive men to
simple faith. "Therefore to whom turn I,
but to Thee, the Ineffable Name? Maker
and Builder, Thou, of houses not built with
hands!" We are the work of a Creator who

may be trusted. It is he who has made us, and makes us, and not we ourselves. In the meantime, that particular difficulty is not a pressing one. It seems likely that for a good many generations to come we shall have plenty of evil in ourselves and in the circumstances of the world to struggle with. It may be that we have not now a smooth time before us. We cannot say that wars have ceased ; we *can* say that when war occurs it is likely to be more awful than ever. There are chances that men may make hurried experiments in the art of extinguishing poverty, and may have to learn wisdom through a poverty not lessened but increased. Growing unbelief may produce a growing laxity of life, and if it does the laxity will most surely produce decay, and the decay will produce suffering, and the populations of men living by nature will be shaken out of their ease. Not laxity, but tension, is what the Divine Trainer demands in the spiritual muscle of those whom he sends into the arena.

Faith in the righteous Creator makes our social duty sufficiently clear to us. Whatever the future may have in store for us, we have to submit ourselves to His guidance so far as

we can apprehend it, and to accept His will
so far as we can learn it, as our supreme law.
We are his instruments, to work with him
for his ends; and he is the power which
brings order out of confusion, a kosmos out
of a chaos. Wherever order is, there is God.
And the highest order we know is that of
spiritual beings adjusted to each other by
spiritual ties, fulfilling their mutual relations
with conscious intelligence and happiness.
Our task is to do all that in us lies to honour
and to realise this order. Where we see
friction and misery, there is something wrong
for us to mend — that is, to help God in
mending[1]—to the best of our power. And
our yearning thought is always to be set
primarily upon the spiritual life of those
whom we would raise, of the men and women
and children who are dislocated and stunted
and pining limbs of the social body; and
therefore upon self-control, goodwill, mutual
respect, the common pursuit of the common
good. To the Christian these virtues are

[1] "Then said his Lordship: 'Well, God mend all!'
'Nay, by God, Donald, we must help him to mend it!' said
the other."—RUSHWORTH (Sir David Ramsay and Lord
Rea, in 1630). Motto prefixed to Carlyle's *Latter-Day
Pamphlets*.

rooted in the filial knowledge of God; and
he must therefore desire, as the best thing,
that a living and fruitful faith in the Son
who reveals the Father may be deepened
and extended. It is evident to him that,
just in proportion as people become, not by
profession, but inwardly and in simplicity,
Christian, the necessary virtues of social life
begin to flourish, righteousness is seen to
prevail, and friction and misery are relieved.
The bettering of outward social conditions is
a promised reward of the service of righteousness. Being Christians, it is impossible that
we should not, whilst thinking chiefly of
righteousness and peace and joy in the Holy
Ghost, desire heartily also outward comfort
and prosperity. And we can see that the
things of this earth are not merely allowed to
be the reward, but are also the instruments
and materials, of spiritual advancement.
Men are only trained through being tried:
thus much can we see of the Divine methods,
whilst much remains mysterious and appar-
ently contradictory to us. That appetite for
pleasant things which, to the agnostic, is the
only impelling human force, is to us a real
and inextinguishable element in the Divine

creation. To suppose that we can leave it out of account, to treat it as exclusively evil, is an error for which our calculations will suffer. All attempts to eliminate competition, which is the working of the self-protecting and self-furthering appetite in human beings, from the business-dealings of the world, have a sentence of futility upon them. This appetite is a natural force, sure to assert itself, visibly productive of desirable results. But, as the fleshly appetites—the absence of which would be a symptom of death, which are indispensable to the growth and health of the body—need to be kept in subjection; as to allow them to be dominant is to give up the life of the spirit, and the training and success of spiritual life turn upon a continued defiance of the authority of these appetites; so it is with competition in the industrial and commercial world. It is not to be extirpated; it *is* to be subjected. The principle and method of competition will never be superseded by a system of government arranging for every one how he is to work and to be made comfortable : the trial of just men and just nations will be how they can deal with one another honourably and fairly, with consideration by each of the advantage of others as well as of his own ; as St. Paul said, "not looking each of you to his own things, but each of you *also* to the things of others." That is the splendid field of human probation for the immediate future. To lay down that no one is to possess any goods which he can call his own would be.a mistake, sure to end in failure ; but to gain possessions honourably, to keep them firmly under the foot, to be a true steward of them, to use them nobly and wisely for the general good, to give them up joyfully when a call to such sacrifice is heard, —that is the duty and the dignity of the spiritual man. That the application of spiritual principles to human life in our day will tend towards the equalising of classes, and the honouring of every man, and the removing of occasions of grudging and dis- content, as well as towards a more cheerfully acknowledged supremacy of ever-improving law, is what Christians will be constrained to acknowledge and will understand with thank- fulness. The Scripture has not said in vain, " Let the brother of low degree glory in his high estate, and the rich in that he is made low." The adjusting of individuals to their places, and the perfecting of each in his place, with an eye to the common well-being, cannot be imagined as going on without much modifying of our inherited customs and arrangements; and the changes to be made will evidently be to some extent of the kind which are now kindling the aspirations of the working classes and their advocates.

But will God grant to us that the "dim" innumerable multitudes, whose minds are now touched by the ferment of not unchristian hopes, may have some discernment given to them of the true glory of society, of the true dignity of the individual? Ah, how much lies in the answer to that question! It would seem that throughout the common populations of Christian lands there is much Christian sentiment diffused,—hearty impulses of compassion and good nature, a strong sense of fellowship with their kind, a prompt readiness to take the side of the weak; but that their slight and wavering hold of what has been disclosed in Jesus Christ of God's action and purposes, and the weakening of the habit (where it is not entirely lost) of appealing reverently and directly to God, leave them without clear ideals, without the needful sway of Divine spiritual authority over their hearts and imaginations, and without the guidance which would best lead them on their way into the unknown future. They are too apt to listen to those whose worship is of the empty idol Equality, and to believe that the beginning and end of justice is to take from those who have more and give to those who have less. If their eyes could be opened to a higher idea of justice than that of reduced inequality, to a nobler ideal of society than that in which the poor have an increased share of the good things of this life, we might hope to see the promises of the future more richly and more speedily realised. The light from heaven for which we look is essentially that of knowledge and harmonious fellow-work and happiness; the darkness which keeps it from us is that of greed and pride and ill-will and ignorance in any class and in any heart. May God hasten the time when his thankful children shall be able to say of every part of this earth as well as of the heaven which broods over it —The darkness is past! The true light now shineth!

Printed by R. & R. CLARK, *Edinburgh.*

MESSRS. MACMILLAN AND CO.'S PUBLICATIONS.

SERMONS BY J. B. LIGHTFOOT, D.D.,
Late Bishop of Durham.

Crown 8vo. Cloth. 6s. each.

ORDINATION ADDRESSES AND COUNSELS TO CLERGY.

CAMBRIDGE SERMONS.

SERMONS PREACHED IN ST. PAUL'S.

LEADERS IN THE NORTHERN CHURCH. Second Edition. With Additional Sermon by Dr. WESTCOTT, Bishop of Durham.

BY THE LATE DEAN CHURCH.

Just ready, Fourth Thousand. 8vo. 12s. 6d. *net.*

THE OXFORD MOVEMENT. Twelve Years, 1833-1845. By the Very Rev. R. W. CHURCH, M.A., D.C.L., late Dean of St. Paul's, etc.

Crown 8vo. Cloth. 7s. 6d.

THE GIFTS OF CIVILISATION, and other Sermons and Lectures delivered at Oxford and in St. Paul's Cathedral. [*New Edition, just published.*

Crown 8vo. 4s. 6d.

DISCIPLINE OF THE CHRISTIAN CHARACTER, and other Sermons. Second Edition.

Crown 8vo. 4s. 6d.
ADVENT SERMONS, 1885.
Crown 8vo. 6s.

HUMAN LIFE AND ITS CONDITIONS. Sermons preached before the University of Oxford in 1876-1878, with Three Ordination Sermons.

NEW BOOK BY THE BISHOP OF DURHAM.

Globe 8vo. 6s.

ESSAYS IN THE HISTORY OF RELIGIOUS THOUGHT IN THE WEST. By BROOKE FOSS WESTCOTT, D.D., D.C.L., Lord Bishop of Durham, Honorary Fellow of Trinity and King's College, Cambridge.

BY THE SAME AUTHOR.

8vo. Cloth.

THE EPISTLE TO THE HEBREWS. The Greek Text, with Notes and Essays. 14s.

THE EPISTLES OF ST. JOHN. The Greek Text, with Notes. Second Edition. 12s. 6d.

Crown 8vo. Cloth.

GENERAL SURVEY OF THE HISTORY OF THE CANON OF THE NEW TESTAMENT DURING THE FIRST FOUR CENTURIES. Sixth Edition. 10s. 6d.
INTRODUCTION TO THE STUDY OF THE FOUR GOSPELS. Seventh Edition. 10s. 6d.
THE GOSPEL OF THE RESURRECTION. Sixth Edition. 6s.
THE BIBLE IN THE CHURCH. Tenth Edition. 18mo. 4s. 6d.
THE CHRISTIAN LIFE, MANIFOLD AND ONE. 2s. 6d.
ON THE RELIGIOUS OFFICE OF THE UNIVERSITIES. Sermons. 4s. 6d.
THE REVELAION OF THE RISEN LORD. Fourth Edition. 6s.
THE HISTORIC FAITH. Third Edition. 6s.

THE REVELATION OF THE FATHER. 6s.
CHRISTUS CONSUMMATOR. Second Edition. 6s.
SOME THOUGHTS FROM THE ORDINAL. 1s. 6d.
SOCIAL ASPECTS OF CHRISTIANITY. 6s.
GIFTS FOR MINISTRY. Addresses to Candidates for Ordination. 1s. 6d.
THE VICTORY OF THE CROSS. Sermons preached during Holy Week, 1888, in Hereford Cathedral. 3s. 6d.
FROM STRENGTH TO STRENGTH. Three Sermons (In Memoriam J. B. D.) 2s.
THOUGHTS ON REVELATION AND LIFE. Selections from the Writings of Canon WESTCOTT. Edited by Rev. S. PHILLIPS. 6s.

MACMILLAN AND CO., LONDON.

www.ingramcontent.com/pod-product-compliance
Lightning Source LLC
Chambersburg PA
CBHW030904050726
47500CB00009B/1018